WHEN MAN MEETS MONSTER . . .

Jupiter Monk had almost reached the safety of the hangar when he saw it—a huge batlike creature, seven feet tall, bright red, fangs all too visible. Its multifaceted eyes fell on Monk, and it emitted an ominous gutteral noise.

"Back off," said Monk.

The creature twitched its cupped ears and bared its fangs.

Staring at this killer creature from his childhood nightmares, Monk started to back away, flexing his knees to meet an attack as the creature slowly advanced toward him . . .

THE WILD ALIEN TAMER

Tales of the Galactic Midway #3

by
MIKE RESNICK

A SIGNET BOOK
NEW AMERICAN LIBRARY
TIMES MIRROR

To Carol, as always,

And to John Guidry,
for friendship above and beyond the call

NAL BOOKS ARE AVAILABLE AT QUANTITY DISCOUNTS WHEN USED TO PROMOTE PRODUCTS OR SERVICES. FOR INFORMATION PLEASE WRITE TO PREMIUM MARKETING DIVISION, THE NEW AMERICAN LIBRARY, INC., 1633 BROADWAY, NEW YORK, NEW YORK 10019.

SIGNET TRADEMARK REG. U.S. PAT. OFF. AND FOREIGN COUNTRIES
REGISTERED TRADEMARK—MARCA REGISTRADA
HECHO EN CHICAGO, U.S.A.

SIGNET, SIGNET CLASSICS, MENTOR, PLUME, MERIDIAN AND NAL BOOKS are published by The New American Library, Inc.,
1633 Broadway, New York, New York 10019

First Printing, July, 1983

1 2 3 4 5 6 7 8 9

PRINTED IN THE UNITED STATES OF AMERICA

1.

Thaddeus Flint stopped two of the alien crewmen as they hauled the rectangular slab of granite down the cargo ship's gangplank.

"What the hell is *that* supposed to be?" he demanded.

"Check the manifest," was the bored reply, filtered through a translating mechanism.

"Just lay the damned thing down and let me take a look at it."

They shrugged and did as he ordered, and he stood, hands on hips, cigarette dangling from his lips, staring at it.

> BRUNO
> Born 1973, Earth
> Died 1984, Pollux IV
> THE MEANEST, DUMBEST, UGLIEST
> SON OF A BITCH EVER TO COME
> OUT OF THE KLONDIKE
> R.I.P.

"Strictly speaking," commented Flint dryly, "he was a son of a bear."

The two crewmen stared at him blankly.

"Don't know what I'm talking about, do you?" he said.

"No, sir."

He sighed. "Well, why the hell should I expect a pink lizard with a goiter condition to know what a bear is?" he muttered. He turned his eyes to the distant horizon, found a moon that didn't belong there, looked up, and spotted six more of varying sizes and colors.

"What the hell kind of a world has seven moons out at noon?" he asked.

"This is Girodus II," said one of the crewmen.

"Spare me the details," said Flint sardonically. He took a salt tablet to help him cope with the heat and humidity, and an adrenaline capsule to ease the feeling of strain caused by the planet's somewhat higher gravity. Now, he thought, if only I could take a pill to get rid of idiot cargo hands, alien tank towns, brown grass and yellow water and too goddamned many moons. . . .

He turned back to the unloading area and looked around until he saw a tall, cadaverous, hairless being with blue skin, orange eyes, and oddly jointed limbs.

"Mr. Ahasuerus!" he bellowed.

"Yes, Mr. Flint?" said the blue man, walking over.

"What's the story on this thing?" asked Flint, gesturing toward the headstone.

"Ah! It arrived!" said Mr. Ahasuerus happily.

"Yes, it arrived," repeated Flint. "My Ferris wheel didn't arrive. My replacement part for the cotton-candy machine didn't arrive. But someone, somewhere, has seen fit to send *The Ahasuerus and Flint Traveling Carnival and Sideshow* a goddamned tombstone for a dead animal. You wouldn't happen to know why, would you?"

"Bruno was the last of the original animals from Earth," replied the blue man. "It seemed a fitting memorial."

"It did, did it?"

"Yes," said the blue man, nodding. "Mr. Monk himself suggested the inscription after explaining that such memorials are common on Earth."

"Did Mr. Monk also explain that such memorials, on those very rare occasions when they are given to animals, are placed on the grave of the deceased, and that the fucking bear is buried three hundred light-years from here?"

"No," admitted Mr. Ahasuerus, looking distressed. "No, he didn't."

"Figures," muttered Flint. "Where is he?"

"Waiting for his new animals, I should imagine."

"Well, let's hope this batch is better than the last. By the way, how much did that piece of rock set us back?"

"Three thousand credits," replied the blue man.

"I don't know from credits. How much is that in American money?"

"You really should make some effort to learn those conversion tables I made up for you."

"Skip the lecture," said Flint. "How much?"

"About twenty-four hundred dollars," replied Mr. Ahasuerus. "Of course, that's 1982 Constant dollars. I have no idea what inflation may have done to—"

"Twenty-four hundred dollars?" yelled Flint. "You tell Monk that it's coming out of his pay!" He snuffed out his cigarette and lit another one. "Jesus H. Christ! I spend the better part of two years turning this show into a paying proposition, and the second I turn my back you start okaying money for tombstones!"

"We can afford it," said Mr. Ahasuerus calmly.

"Pull a couple more stunts like this and I'll bet we can even afford a matching one for a bald blue skeleton," said Flint. He paused for a moment and emitted a deep sigh. "Look, I don't mean to lose my temper with you. But after two years you ought to know that all carnies are liars."

"Including you?" asked Mr. Ahasuerus, pulling his lips back from his teeth in his equivalent of a smile.

"Including me. But I'm selective about it: I just lie to the marks. Monk and the rest, they'll lie to anyone." He looked down at the granite marker again. "Oh, well, see if there's anything resembling a graveyard around here and plant it."

"And if not?"

"Dump it into Monk's room and let *him* worry about it."

Flint spent the next half hour supervising the rest of the unloading, discovered that he had been sent a ride that had been earmarked for the humanoids of Canphor VI and had not received the one he had ordered to accommodate the elephantine beings of Girodus II, had the crew reload it into the ship, and sent off still another nasty message to the Corporation. He did receive three tons of sugar, but with his cotton-candy machine out of order he didn't see much use for it, and reloaded it as well.

Finally, sweating profusely and wondering why Mr. Ahasuerus seemed to pick only exceptionally hot worlds or frigid ones, he clambered down the gangplank, lit another cigarette, took his shirt off, and signed a number of receipts after having one of the aliens translate them for him.

He was about to go to the carnival ship's galley for a cold beer—which, he knew, would be lukewarm and taste like weak tea—when a small hunchbacked human approached him.

"What's wrong now?" asked Flint.

"Nothing," replied the hunchback, speaking with a severe stammer. "I just thought I'd see if there was any mail."

"That's very thoughtful of you, Tojo," said Flint dryly. "You think the United States Post Office might be making deliveries out here, do you?"

"We have thirty-two aliens working for us, Thaddeus," said Tojo. "Most of them come from the Community of Worlds. I thought they might have some letters from home."

"Yeah? Well, if the mail service out here is anything like the cargo service, the letters are probably somewhere in the Andromeda galaxy by now. There's probably a real good reason why the Corporation hasn't gone bankrupt yet, but I sure as hell can't come up with it."

"We didn't get our Ferris wheel," said Tojo. It was not a question.

"Among other things." Flint raised his gaze to the heavens, shielding his eyes from the glare of the binary star. "I wonder how things are going in Vermont. At least we didn't have to readapt the rides every time we moved to a new town." He took another puff of his cigarette and coughed. "And a man could get a decent smoke."

"You've been complaining about the cigarettes for two years, Thaddeus."

"The ship's robots have been making lousy cigarettes for two years," replied Flint. "Next year I'll have been complaining for three years."

"There *is* an alternative," said Tojo softly.

"You tell me what it is again and you just may get whacked on the side of the head."

Tojo sighed and remained silent.

"Did you see that goddamned tombstone?" said Flint at last, lighting up yet another cigarette and coughing again.

"Yes," replied the hunchback. "I thought it was a very touching gesture."

"Monk hated the bear and the bear hated Monk. What's so touching about that?" demanded Flint.

"I take it the tombstone wasn't your idea?"

"What do you think?" He paused. "Where the hell *is* Clyde Beatty, anyway?"

"His new animals have been unloaded," said Tojo. "I imagine he's with them."

"Oh, well," said Flint with a shrug. "I saw the robots making up a keg of beer this morning. I suppose I ought to let it age another half hour, just to be civilized about it. Let's go on over and see what he's picked out this time."

They walked down the Midway, past the Skillo games and the Fascination booths and the Three-Card Monte tables and the Bozo cage, past the Wax Museum and the concession stands, past the specialty tent where Billybuck Dancer put on his Wild West Show Three Times Nightly, past the makeshift wrestling ring where the carnival offered 50-Credits-50 to anyone who could stay five minutes with Julius Squeezer, their green-skinned and slightly reptilian muscleman from far Antares. They went out to the little circle of trailers and vehicles that were perhaps two hundred yards beyond the various rides, and finally they came to a training cage, some fifty feet in diameter, around which a number of the carny workers had gathered.

Standing by the door was Jupiter Monk, sweat pouring down from his thinning hair, his huge handlebar mustache drooping in the heat. The burly animal trainer was dressed all in khaki, and was absently fingering a small "popper" whip, designed more to startle than to harm.

Standing directly opposite Monk, on the far side of the cage, was a slender blond man dressed in denim pants and jacket and wearing a felt Stetson. He stood so motionless that Flint didn't see him at first, and when at last he did he walked over to him.

"Riding shotgun?" asked Flint.

"Yep," replied Billybuck Dancer.

"Do me a favor. If there's any trouble and you have to use that thing"—Flint gestured toward the pistol that the Dancer had tucked in his holster—"shoot Monk."

The Dancer chuckled. "I heard about the tombstone. Jupiter said he thought you were going to be a little upset."

"An understatement," muttered Flint. He turned and looked at the three crates that had been wheeled up to the cage. "Why the hell can't he work 'em into his act gradually, like any normal person? By my count you've had to kill five animals so far."

"First of all, he ain't *got* no act now that Bruno and the cats are dead," said the young man in his gentle Texas drawl. "And second, he's only got twenty-four hours to approve of the animals or send 'em back. Would you rather cart some animal around that he can't work with?"

"Just the same, I'm out sixty thousand dollars on dead animals," said Flint. "Can't you get the robots to rig your gun with tranquilizer darts?"

"Sure," said the Dancer pleasantly. "But it'd kill 'em anyway. These ain't lions and tigers, Thaddeus."

Flint was about to reply, thought better of it, and turned his attention to the ring, where one of the crates was being unloaded. Monk had the robots place it just inside the door. Then, locking the cage again, he pressed the release on the crate, and a small purple catlike animal bounded out, hissing furiously.

Monk snorted in disgust, walked into the cage, herded the snarling little animal up against the bars, darted a hand out and picked it up by the scruff of the neck before it could bite or scratch him, and tossed it back into the crate, cursing a blue streak the whole time.

"What the hell was *that* supposed to be?" demanded Flint, walking around to the door.

"It was *supposed* to be the most vicious carnivore on Belthar III," said Monk with a laugh. "Hell, for all I know it is."

"Well, you're the guy who picked it."

"I picked it from a holograph that your Corporation buddy Kargennian sent me," said Monk patiently. "The little bastard is exactly as represented, too—except that Kargennian never said what its size was. I thought I was getting something about four hundred pounds." He laughed again. "I've seen bigger beagles."

"Wasn't there some kind of spec sheet with the holograph?" asked Flint.

"I got enough trouble reading English."

"You don't seem to have much trouble dictating it," remarked Flint wryly.

"The tombstone, right?" Monk put on an angelic

face and smiled. "It ain't *my* fault that your partner hasn't got a sense of humor." He turned to one of the robots. "Take this one back to the ship, and haul the next crate in here."

"My partner's lack of a sense of humor is going to cost you a couple of thousand dollars," continued Flint.

"What the hell do I care?" replied Monk. "There ain't an awful lot to spend it on out here, in case you hadn't noticed. Now, why don't you stand back—unless you feel a serious need to work the next animal, that is."

Flint stood away from the door as the second crate was placed inside the cage and Monk released the lock.

Nothing emerged.

"Antisocial son of a bitch, ain't he?" said Monk.

He walked into the cage and stood in front of the crate. Whatever was inside uttered an ominous growl.

"Well, at least it isn't dead," remarked Flint.

Monk locked the crate again and told a robot to remove it.

"Don't you even want to see what you've got?" asked Flint.

Monk shook his head. "What I've got in there is a mess of trouble. We're returning it."

"Without trying to work with it?" demanded Flint.

"Thaddeus, I've only got twenty-four hours to accept one of these animals or reject it. Any animal that won't come out of its cage is likely to feel so scared and so trapped that all it's going to do is attack out of fear. Now, maybe it's a temporary condition and maybe it ain't, but unless you feel like carting around a twenty-thousand-dollar animal that we may never be able to use, it's my opinion that we ought to return it. I guarantee that I won't be able to find out in one day's time whether I can work with it or not."

Flint shrugged. "You're the trainer."

"Damn it, Thaddeus!" said Monk. "Don't you think I *want* an animal I can work with? I took a lion, a bear, and two leopards with me when we left Earth. My act is buried on four goddamned worlds that I can't even pick out in the night sky. We've tried fourteen animals in the last six months. I sent nine back and the Dancer had to kill the other five. I'd sell my soul for another Simba, or even something like Bruno."

Flint made no reply, and Monk directed the robot to move the third crate into the ring. When he released the catch a large grayish animal, wolflike in appearance but far larger, stalked out. It strode once around the ring, seemingly unperturbed by its surroundings, walked slowly toward the crate from which it had emerged, and suddenly screamed and hurled itself directly toward the Dancer. It bounced back off the bars of the cage, rolled over twice, and then continued walking calmly around and around the ring.

"Well, he's got possibilities," said Monk.

"And an appetite," added Flint dryly.

"I like his feet," said Monk, studying the animal.

"Oh? Why?"

"Retractable claws. That means he ought to be able to catch things."

"Like animal trainers?" asked Flint.

"He doesn't need claws to kill a man," said Monk. "I wonder what the hell his natural prey is? Must be something half again as big as a buffalo."

"And you're going to play catch with him?"

"Not this morning," said Monk with a smile. "I'm just going to get acquainted with him. Reminds me of a dog I used to own."

"He was bigger than any dog you ever owned the day he was born," said Flint.

"My friend the optimist," muttered Monk. He waited for the animal to reach the far side of the ring, then quickly walked through the door, holding a small metal chair in one hand and his whip in the other.

"Hi, Shep," he said gently.

The animal turned and glared at him, and Monk stood motionless, the chair positioned just ahead of him. The animal moved to its left, and Monk turned slowly, keeping the chair between them. It stopped again, growled once, and began walking back to its right. Monk pivoted to face it.

Then, suddenly, it took a single bound toward Monk, stopping about eight feet away as Monk cracked his whip. Flint shot a quick glance at the Dancer, who now had his pistol out and trained on the animal, then looked back at Monk, who raised the chair a little higher and took a tentative step forward.

The animal snarled and backed away, and Monk advanced another step. The animal retreated again, and Monk spent the next five minutes forcing it to move where he wanted it. Twice the animal charged at him, and twice the sound of the whip made it come to a stop.

"Tojo!" Monk called.

"Yes?" said the hunchback, shuffling up to the cage.

"Go to one of the game booths and bring back a couple of toys. Balls, if you can find them."

Tojo headed off to the Midway, and Monk continued moving the animal. After another three minutes he put the chair down and began working it solely by gliding his whip along the ground.

"Quick learner," remarked Flint.

"While we're waiting for Tojo, have one of the robots bring me a stool," said Monk. "One of the ones I used for the cats."

Flint issued the order, and a moment later Monk had set the aluminum stool up next to the door. Then he moved the animal around the ring to where the stool was, and began backing it up until finally, with a sound that was halfway between a sigh and a snarl, it jumped onto the stool. The crowd around the ring applauded—

—and the animal went berserk.

It leaped off the stool, knocking Monk over in the process, charged straight for the Dancer, bounced off the cage bars, leaped up in the air, split its muzzle open on the top of the rigging, and began racing around the perimeter of the cage.

"Don't shoot him unless he goes for me!" Monk yelled to the Dancer. He was on his feet, edging his way to the door, and suddenly the animal skidded to a stop and began approaching him very slowly. Monk cracked his whip again, and the animal began racing around the cage once more, foaming at the mouth and dribbling a foul-smelling stream of urine behind itself.

It took another minute to stop, and then Monk finally drove it back and carefully stepped out of the cage.

"What the hell happened?" asked Flint.

"The noise," said Monk, panting heavily and sweating profusely. "The whip scares him a bit, but applause is going to drive him absolutely up a tree."

"Is there anything you can do with him?"

"He's psychotic, Thaddeus. I can put on a show for small and select audiences who promise never to yell or clap their hands, but there's no way he's going to be able to work in the specialty tent. Look at him—he's crapping all over himself."

Flint looked at the huge carnivore trembling in the center of the ring, whining and slowly going to pieces, and shook his head. "I thought we had one this time," he said at last.

"When he calms down I'll get him back to his crate," said Monk, picking up a towel and mopping his face. "I hope no one runs any machines around here in the meantime."

"I'll see to it," said Flint. He passed the order to a couple of the carnies and a robot.

Tojo arrived a minute later, laden down with plastic and hard-rubber balls.

"You didn't say which kind you wanted," he explained, "so I brought a selection."

"You're too late," said Flint. "The fun's over."

"What happened?" asked Tojo, laying the balls down carefully. He looked into the ring. "Did the Dancer have to shoot him?"

Flint shook his head. "Let's just say that he's not real likely to become the next Rin Tin Tin and leave it at that."

"He looks sick," continued the hunchback.

"He'll be okay," said Flint.

"This is stupid," Monk announced at last.

"What is?"

"If there's a dumber way to build an animal act, I sure as hell don't know what it is. Thaddeus, you've got to let me take a ship and go out myself. I can't put an act together by mail."

"I've told you why you can't," began Flint.

"Yeah, but that was different. I still had Bruno, and you needed me in the specialty tent. Well, now I've got nothing. You can either pay me a hundred grand a year to hold targets for the Dancer, or you can let me put together an act that'll draw some customers."

"What makes you think you can *get* anything worthwhile?" said Flint.

"You think Gunther Gebel-Williams is the only trainer that ever lived who can wrap a tiger around his shoulders?" said Monk. "Hell, I used to pull food right out of Simba's mouth! But *I* got to choose the animal. Even this cowering hulk in the ring here—if I'd had him as a baby, he'd be pulling better crowds than the Dancer."

"*Nothing* outdraws the Dancer," said Flint firmly. "Still, you've got a point. You're making too damned much money to sit on your hands, and there's no way we can send you home." He paused. "Where would you start looking?"

"Just program a ship to take me to a few worlds that have zoos, fix me up with a translating device, and give me a line of credit," said Monk. "I'll take it from there."

"Let me talk to the skeleton about it," said Flint. He turned to leave. "Stick around until Kazan of the North has calmed down enough to put him back into his crate, and then help out with the games."

"Is there anything you want *me* to do, Thaddeus?" asked Tojo.

"You mean besides checking the concession goods against the manifest, changing the lighting in the specialty tent, and making sure the animals get back on the cargo ship?" asked Flint. "Yeah. Why don't you put the balls back where you got 'em from before someone comes along and swipes 'em?"

Flint walked back through the Midway to the huge spaceship, stopped off in the mess hall long enough to pick up a beer, and took the elevator up to his partner's office on the top level. He entered without knocking, as usual, walked over to a couch of unearthly design, and tried unsuccessfully to make himself comfortable.

The blue man was facing one of the walls, staring at an oddly distorted print while holding another out in front of him. His ever-present cup of coffee, to which he had become addicted during his brief stay on Earth, sat on his desk.

"Ah, Mr. Flint," he said, looking up. "Which of these do you think looks better here?" He turned and held the print up for Flint to see.

"I can't say that either one of them makes a lot of sense. I just hope to hell nothing in the galaxy actually looks like that."

"You disapprove of them?" asked the blue man mildly.

"Mr. Ahasuerus, I've been coming up here every day for more than two years, and every day you've been playing with some new painting or drawing or holograph that's even weirder than the last one," replied Flint. "Even *you* can't take this junk seriously."

"I assure you, these are works of art." said the blue man.

Flint snorted. "Art is fat naked women. The rest is just so much hogwash."

"Stated with your customary sophistication," commented Mr. Ahasuerus in an amused tone of voice. "And now, to what do I owe the pleasure of this visit?"

"I just got back from the training cage."

"Did we have any luck with Monk's animals?"

"Not so's you'd notice it."

Mr. Ahasuerus sighed heavily. "I feared as much. You know, Mr. Flint, this is simply not the way to build an animal act."

"Someone's been talking to you," said Flint with a smile.

"For quite some time now," admitted the blue man. "I have come to the conclusion that he is correct."

"Me too," agreed Flint. "*You* tell him, though. I don't think I could stand to watch him gloat."

"If you wish."

Flint picked up an oddly shaped and totally incomprehensible artifact from a hardwood table and toyed with it. "Where do you plan to send him?" he asked at last.

"I thought *you* might have some suggestions," said Mr. Ahasuerus.

"You mean printable ones?" Flint took a sip of his beer and made a face. "God, this stuff is terrible!" He wiped his mouth off, grimaced, and took another swallow. "See if you can't find something really off the beaten track—maybe a couple of worlds that aren't even members of your Community."

"Is there any particular reason for that?" inquired the blue man. "And please be careful with that artifact. It's quite irreplaceable."

"I should hope so," said Flint, placing it back on the table with obvious distaste. "I'd hate to think there were two of them floating around the universe." He looked up at his partner. "By this time Monk's seen just about everything Kargennian and the others have to offer. Maybe he can find something more to his taste out in the sticks." He paused. "How much do we plan to spend?"

"For a good act, the sky's the limit."

"Don't tell *him* that; he'll take you at your word."

"Shall we say a hundred thousand credits?" offered Mr. Ahasuerus.

"Shall we translate that into *real* money?" replied Flint wearily.

"About eighty-two thousand dollars."

"That's too much."

"We're taking in twice that much every night," responded the blue man.

"I know," said Flint. "Not bad for a joint that was almost bankrupt a year and a half ago—especially when you consider that they change the rules on us every time we hit a new world." He shrugged. "Okay, eighty-two thousand dollars it is." He took another sip of his beer. "You know, if we give a guy like Monk that much money and no time limit, we may never see him again. Tell him that wherever he is and whatever he's doing, the robot pilot is bringing the ship home six months to the minute from now, empty or full."

"Do you mean it?" asked the blue man.

"Of course not. But as long as Monk believes it, what's the difference?"

"You're an interesting man, Mr. Flint."

"I'll assume that's a compliment, Mr. Ahasuerus," said Flint ironically.

The blue man got to his feet. "I'd better go have a talk with Monk now."

Flint shook his head. "Let him sweat a little. Come on," he added, also rising. "I'll buy you a beer."

"That's a very generous offer," said Mr. Ahasuerus, "but I'm afraid my metabolism doesn't—"

"Neither does mine," interrupted Flint. "But I figure if I make you drink enough of this stuff, you'll see to it that the robots learn how to make it a little better."

"You're all heart, Mr. Flint," said the blue man glumly, as he followed his partner to the elevator.

2.

"They're just a bunch of goddamned seals!"

Jupiter Monk, protected from the howling winds and subzero temperature of Beta Scuti XI by an oversized fur coat, thick gloves and boots, and a plastic face mask, was looking down into an enormous pool from a narrow overhead ramp. The creatures he was observing darted around and under a number of small ice floes, surfacing only for air and to emit an occasional piglike grunt.

"I came seventy light-years out of my way to look at seals!" he repeated incredulously.

"That is not a term I understand, sir," said his guide.

"You don't know what a seal is?" said Monk. "Well, now, just stick your head over the edge of the ramp and look straight down and what you're going to be looking at is a batch of seals. I had a friend called Denny Taylor who went broke on Earth trying to put together a seal act. All they can do is balance stuff on their noses and blow a few notes on a set of horns." He shook his head in amazement. "Seals, for Christ's sake!"

"I assure you that these animals exist nowhere else in the Community of Worlds," said the guide, drawing himself up to his full, if minimal, height. He was mildly humanoid in structure, though his arms and legs seemed too long for the rest of him and his face was incapable of expression.

"Friend, the only difference between your seals and mine is that mine bark like dogs and yours oink like pigs." Monk turned to the guide. "I told you on the goddamned radio that I needed something dangerous."

"They *are* dangerous, sir," answered the guide. "They are carnivores, they are very mobile in their natural environment, they are able to withstand extreme cold, they—"

"I'm freezing to death and you're describing seals to me!" said Monk unbelievingly. "Look, pal, they ain't going to be performing in their natural environment."

"They are not, sir?"

"Not unless I grow a set of fins or gills."

"I had rather assumed you would not be entering the water to work with them."

"Did you also assume that I'm equipped to frolic around in the snow?"

"I doubt it, sir."

"You figure my audiences are a hell of a lot different from me?"

"I hadn't given it any thought, sir," came the reply.

"Well, so as not to put any undue stress on your brain, let me tell you that they ain't. Now, before I freeze my ass off, let's get straight one more time just what it is that I'm looking for. I need a goddamned land-dwelling carnivore. I need something that won't fold up its tent and die the second it gets warm out. I need something that won't take half a day to travel a hundred yards on dry land. I need something that can do more than balance a ball on its nose. Are you following me?"

"Yes," replied the guide. "But I must point out that these are the only carnivores on our planet that fulfill your size requirements."

"Somehow, I ain't exactly surprised," said Monk. "Well, I'd better get back to the ship before I turn into the strangest-looking popsicle you ever saw."

"I could make a price if you were to buy four or more," offered the guide.

"You know, I could have sworn you had ears under all that hair." He stared disbelievingly at the guide. "Look—if I don't want *one* seal, why do you think I want *four* of them?"

"I thought you might be haggling," said the guide. "The limited information we have on Terrans is that they like to drive bargains."

"Yeah? Well, *I* don't. And I ain't a Terran; I'm an Alaskan." He began clambering down off the ramp. "I don't suppose anyone on this world makes a decent cup of coffee?"

"Coffee, sir?"

Monk sighed. "Just get me to the ship."

"You're very amusing, sir," said the guide. "Are all members of your race like you?"

"None of 'em are half as good-looking as me," said Monk. "And most of 'em would have you boiled in oil for bringing them out here just to look at seals. They ain't all as good-natured as I am."

"Oh," replied the guide.

It was the very last thing he said, and shortly thereafter Monk was back aboard his ship, bound for Sabellius III and wondering why it was so difficult to put together an animal act in a universe filled with exotic life forms.

He had landed on Bori IV two months ago, hopeful of finding everything he needed there and cutting short his trip. What he found was impressive, to be sure, and there was no question that they were dangerous and carnivorous. They were also some twenty-five feet at the shoulder, fifty tons in weight, and so incredibly simpleminded as to be totally untrainable. Not that their intelligence mattered all that much; they were also too big to fit into his ship and too expensive to feed, which negated all further considerations.

The second world he had visited, Gamma Delta V, had provided the most interesting animals: amoebalike blobs of protoplasm that could be trained to form themselves into artistic and fascinating shapes. He spent a few days working with them before concluding—reluctantly, because they were very pleasant and quite amenable to training—that while they might have enhanced an art gallery, they just weren't a viable act for a carnival.

He found pretty much what he wanted on Dorillion, the third world he visited. They had four different catlike species of carnivore, ranging from a silver animal barely smaller than a leopard to a huge mottled creature almost twice the size of a lion. They were reasonably intelligent and reasonably trainable—and unreasonably expensive. He radioed Flint and laid out the situation for him—two million credits per animal—and wasn't surprised that Flint felt the prices were outrageous.

He never found out what kind of animals there were on Quantos VIII. Long before he got there he was informed that because of a worldwide plague that had affected their meat animals, *all* their other animals were now being used as food.

The fifth world on his agenda was Voorhite XIV. He didn't land there either, once he found out that it possessed a chlorine atmosphere and that its animals would perish upon contact with oxygen.

Beta Scuti XI was the sixth of the ten worlds Mr. Ahasuerus had programmed into the ship's navigational computer, and as he took off from it on the long journey to Sabellius III he found himself seriously wondering if he would *ever* find replacements for Bruno and Simba and the leopards. Monk had never liked being confined in close quarters, and his added worries about the act served only to make him more uncomfortable than usual during this leg of the voyage.

After spending a few hours trying to concentrate on some books he had borrowed from Tojo—he had taken twenty-seven volumes and hadn't made it to page 30 of any of them—he let himself into the cargo hold for what had become his daily calisthenic session. It had taken him perhaps ten seconds during his first day in space to realize that he didn't *know* any calisthenics, and he had created a regimen based on his remembrances of the warming-up exercises he had seen during pro football pre-game shows on Sunday afternoons. Then one day he had turned off the gravity controls and practiced "swimming" through the air; it hadn't worked quite the way he had anticipated, but he had kept in some semblance of physical shape by pushing off from one wall to the next, not unlike a giant bullfrog. At first, his sessions lasted only fifteen minutes—after all, forty-three-year-old animal tamers didn't use the same muscles as defensive linemen or bullfrogs—but he had gradually worked up to an hour at a time, two periods a day. This, added to sixty minutes of bored browsing through the books and eight hours of sleep, left him thirteen hours a day in which to fight the overwhelming boredom of solitary spaceflight. He fondly remembered Pac-Man and Asteroids from the local arcades in Vermont and tried to jury-rig his cabin's computer for some simple games; the only result was that the hot water in his bathroom no longer worked and the temperature in his compartment fell six degrees.

So he had long conversations with the robot pilot (which, having no voice, never disagreed with him) and sang bawdy ballads at the top of his lungs and made up new anecdotes to go along with the thousands he could dredge up from his colorful past at a moment's notice. He created two all-time all-star baseball teams, one managed by John McGraw and the other by Casey Stengel, and from his imaginary announcer's booth called every pitch of a seven-game World Series. He created a twelve-horse field with every fabulous thoroughbred from Man o' War and Equipoise to Ruffian and Seattle Slew, and had them race at every distance from six furlongs to two miles, then did it again on muddy tracks, and finally started having his winners carry increasingly higher weights during the rematches. He envisioned every play of a tennis match between Bill Tilden and John McEnroe, and then, because he was still bored and didn't like McEnroe very much anyway, had them play again after inflicting McEnroe with hemorrhoids. He verbally rewrote the ending to *Casablanca* and the beginning to *Citizen Kane*, he created a *Maltese Falcon* in which Sam Spade didn't send the girl over and a *Wizard of Oz* in which the Munchkins raped both Dorothy and the Wicked Witch of the West.

That got him all the way up to the second world. Then he *really* had to go to work.

Since leaving Beta Scuti XI he had replayed the first sixteen Super Bowls and rewritten every Sydney Greenstreet/Peter Lorre movie he could remember, and was just about to mentally referee a three-way shootout between Hoot Gibson, Bob Steele, and Clint Eastwood (to even things up a bit, he had decided to make Eastwood wear a patch over his left eye), when suddenly the robot pilot applied the ship's braking mechanisms. Half a minute later, as he was painfully picking himself up from the floor, a small sign lit up over the door of his cabin suggesting that he might find it expedient to connect his safety harness and secure all loose objects in his general vicinity.

He did as directed, picking up yet another of Tojo's books, belatedly discovered that it contained some pretty spicy sex scenes he had overlooked, and was avidly reading it when another sign—and a very noticeable bump—told him that the ship had touched down. He unstrapped himself, turned on his computer, found a complex readout of the planet's gravity and atmosphere that he didn't understand and a sign saying NO PROTECTIVE SUIT REQUIRED that he did, walked to the hatch, opened it, and stepped out into the warm, rather muggy Sabellian air. He breathed in deeply and grimaced; either they had fertilized the field around the spaceport recently, or he was going to have one hell of a difficult time adjusting to the smell of this place. He took a shallow breath to see if it made a difference, and was not surprised to find out that it didn't.

Off in the distance he could see a truly impressive mountain range (or else it was a lot closer than he thought and therefore not so impressive, not that he particularly cared). A river of blue-green water ran placidly along the outskirts of the spaceport, and he decided that whoever had designed the landing field either didn't worry too much about contaminating the water or didn't drink it in the first place.

The spaceport itself was unimpressive, as most of them were. He had been raised on science fiction films and pulp magazines, and had envisioned—as had all the carnies—an unending series of futuristic cities and wonders spanning the length of the galaxy. In point of fact, he reflected, most of the worlds he had seen resembled nothing more than the outskirts of Indianapolis. This current one, and its spaceport, bore an uncanny similarity to Springfield, Missouri.

It was obvious that no passenger ships ever took off or landed here, for while there was a small control tower he could find nothing remotely resembling a passenger terminal. The landing field itself was perhaps half a mile in diameter, and currently held only nine small ships, including his own. There was a beat-up hangar about a quarter of a mile away, just off the edge of the strip, and both the strip and the hangar looked as if they had seen not just better days but better centuries.

Three hundred yards to his right was a takeoff shaft, which was nothing more than a circle of heat-resistant webbing strung out over a deep hole which theoretically contained the heat and flames from departing spaceships. The scars extending for hundreds of feet in all directions implied that the shaft needed to be deeper, or at least farther away from the stationary ships.

An odd-looking bird with leathery wings and dull-gray plumage flew overhead, croaking hoarsely. He watched it for a moment, then shrugged and lowered himself to the ground. He had expected his contact to be waiting for him, but as far as he could tell the field was all but deserted. There were a couple of tan pandalike beings working on one of the ships, but they paid no attention to him, and finally he began walking across the landing strip to the hangar, studying the tall grasses surrounding the spaceport and reluctantly concluding that they didn't look recently fertilized.

He had almost reached the hangar when a door receded and a huge, batlike creature emerged. It had a foreshortened face, not unlike a bulldog or a boxer, with a pronounced underbite and very visible fangs. Both its hands and its feet possessed prehensile thumbs, and its wrists and ankles were joined to a very thin flap of membrane.

Its multifaceted eyes fell on Monk, and it emitted an ominous guttural noise.

"Back off," said Monk, activating his translating device.

The creature twitched its cupped ears and bared its fangs.

"I ain't looking for no trouble," said Monk, backing up a step and flexing his knees in case he had to meet an attack.

The creature growled again, made some gesture with its clawlike hand that Monk was unable to interpret, and walked back inside the hangar on its short, stocky legs.

It emerged again a moment later, and this time Monk had a better opportunity to study it. It stood almost seven feet tall, was a flaming red in color, and was covered by short, coarse, thick hair. There was the look of a predator about it, and the fact that it snorted and rumbled as it breathed did not detract from that impression.

It carried something in its left hand, and when it was about five feet away Monk saw that it was a mechanism built along the lines of his own two-way translating device. He had not seriously considered how a killer creature from his childhood nightmares might have gained access to a spaceport hangar, but although he knew the notion to be ridiculous, he was nonetheless greatly relieved to see this obvious sign of sentience.

The creature raised the device to its mouth and spoke into it.

"You are Jupiter Monk, of *The Ahasuerus and Flint Traveling Carnival and Sideshow*?" came the cold, passionless, translated tones.

"The one and only," replied Monk. "That's what I was about to tell you when you ran off."

"Your translating mechanism has not been adjusted to function in my language."

"I notice that *yours* works just dandy for *mine*," said Monk suspiciously. "How come?"

"Mr. Ahasuerus had a member of the Corporation drop this device off here some weeks ago."

"Well, bully for him. I always knew he was good for something." Monk fumbled in his shirt pocket for a moment, then pulled out a crumpled piece of note paper. "You're Braxtos, right?"

"You must be mispronouncing my name rather badly," said the creature. "Even the translator can't make sense out of what you said." It paused. "My name is—"

There was a silence, as the translating device was unable to come up with a human equivalent.

"Win a few, lose a few," muttered Monk. "It didn't come out at this end either. You must have one hell of a tongue-twister."

"I shall assume that you meant no insult, and that the translation was in error," said the creature.

"This may come as a shock to you, or perhaps a pleasant surprise," said Monk, "but I don't know what the hell you're talking about."

"My tongue is not twisted." To support its statement, it pointed to a small insect that was flying near its face, turned toward it, and darted out its tongue and engulfed it.

"Straightest goddamned tongue I ever saw," said Monk devoutly. "And now, if we're all through introducing ourselves and slaughtering innocent insects, is there any chance that I might be able to see the animals?"

"That is why I am here."

"Good. I just hope they look as weird as you do," said Monk. Then he added quickly, "Meaning no offense."

"No offense is taken," replied the creature. "If you will follow me, I shall lead you to my vehicle." It paused, as if considering its next statement. "As long as we are being frank with each other, I wonder if I might make a small request?"

"Shoot."

"Please do not walk too close to me or make any sudden movements."

"Might instinctively go for me with your tongue, huh?"

"No," said the creature. "I am here to show you the animals, and I will do my job—but I must confess that I find your appearance quite terrifying."

"Figures," muttered Monk, slowing his pace.

They soon arrived at an open vehicle—*car* would be the wrong word for it—and sat as far from each other as possible. As they began traveling across the flat, carefully tended fields, Monk noticed that the odor actually intensified once they got away from the spaceport. He tried to ignore it by studying his surroundings, but soon gave it up, as they didn't change much from one mile to the next—except perhaps to look a little more like Indianapolis and a little less like Springfield, which at least had an occasional gorge or gully.

Finally, after about twenty minutes, they began going into the foothills of the mountain range he had seen upon arriving, and he realized that it was indeed much closer and much smaller than he had thought. Still, he was grateful for any change of scenery, no matter how minute, and for his own amusement he tried to guess which of the small variety of trees and shrubs smelled the worst.

About five miles into the foothills the vehicle slowed down, and then turned onto a side road. Another half mile found them before a large fenced area, and the Sabellian punched out a combination on his dashboard's computer panel. A gate slid open, and the vehicle proceeded up a long driveway to a large building which seemed to be made out of some stuccolike substance.

"This is the place?" asked Monk.

"We have arrived," responded the creature.

They clambered out of the vehicle and walked up the gently inclined ramp that led to the front door of the building. Then the Sabellian punched out another combination on a lock by the doorknob, the door slid soundlessly into a wall, and the two of them walked inside.

The place reminded Monk of a zoo, rather than a holding area for the planet's largest animal-exporting firm. There were cages set into all the walls, enclosed entirely in hard plastic, and the polished floor had an antiseptic smell to it.

In the center of the building was a huge, two-story, barred cage—*not* encased in plastic, and stinking of rotting fruit and fresh stool—that was filled with artificial trees and various types of gymnastic equipment: swings, bars, even a set of rings. Sitting with its back propped up against a tree was an animal that looked suspiciously like Monk himself. A closer examination showed that the animal had a protuding lower jaw, a sharply receding forehead, only four toes on each foot, and a little more body hair—but the resemblance was uncanny.

"Shit!" said Monk.

"I beg your pardon," said the batlike creature.

"That was an expletive, not a directive," answered Monk with a wry smile. "Where'd you get that thing?"

"In the jungles of our southern hemisphere," came the reply. "They used to be quite common, but they have been hunted almost to extinction. Though we feed them fruit, they are omnivorous, and have been known to be quite dangerous on occasion." He paused. "Now you see why I viewed your appearance with some initial trepidation."

Monk quickly scanned the other cages. There were seven more manlike animals identical to the one in the middle of the room, and a number of smaller members of the same general family.

"We got a little problem here," he announced at last.

"I assure you they are quite trainable," said his companion.

"I don't doubt it," said Monk. "You got anything else?"

"I am afraid not. I understood that you needed a carnivore or omnivore of these dimensions. Is there something wrong?"

"You might say so," replied Monk. "I'm not collecting for a zoo. I need animals for a carnival act, and to the average untrained eye, these animals could be my brothers."

"I see," said the Sabellian slowly.

"Well, thanks for your time," said Monk. "And if it'll make you feel any better, your looks scared me as much as mine scared you."

"How very gratifying."

"While we're on the subject, I don't suppose you have any carnivores that look like *you*?"

The creature paused and stared at him for a long moment. "Just what is it that your animals are expected to do?"

"Mostly look ferocious," admitted Monk. "And I'll teach 'em to do whatever tricks they're capable of—jumping through hoops, that sort of thing."

"How many worlds do you play in the course of a year?"

"That's pretty much up to Mr. Ahasuerus. I'd guess about fifteen to twenty." He paused. "You got an animal for me?"

"I might have."

"Yeah?"

"What does the job pay?" asked the Sabellian.

"*Pay?*" repeated Monk. "You got it all wrong. I need an animal for my act in—" Suddenly he stopped speaking and a huge smile spread across his face. "Are you saying what I *think* you're saying?"

"It is entirely possible."

"Then what the hell are we standing around here for?" said Monk. "Let's go somewhere where we can break out a bottle or two of really fine drinkin' stuff and talk a little serious business."

"I know just the place," replied the creature, starting off toward the door. Monk, still grinning from ear to ear, fell into step behind it.

3.

Monk sat on the floor of the Sabellian's room, his back propped up against a stucco wall, a huge cigar sticking out the corner of his mouth. He stared at the tall, oddly shaped glass in his hand, took a second tentative sip just to be sure he had analyzed the first one correctly, and looked up at the creature.

"You got any grain alcohol in the place?" he asked at last.

"Have you an abrasion?"

"Why don't you just bring it on over and not worry your head about it?" replied Monk.

The Sabellian shrugged, turned, and left the room, and Monk once again studied his surroundings. He had thought Mr. Ahasuerus' office aboard the carnival ship was strange, but now he realized just how far out of his way the blue man had gone to make his partner and crew feel at home there. Compared to the Sabellian's apartment, it seemed sensible and conservative to the *n*th degree.

There was, for starters, the furniture. Monk had taken one look at it and opted for sitting on the floor—and as he surveyed it again, he was certain he had made the correct decision. Chairs and couches that were made for seven-foot beings with short legs and vestigial wings simply weren't suitable for humans.

Neither, he reflected, was anything else in the room. It had taken his eyes almost a full minute to adjust to the very dim lighting, and the place's color scheme—light gray on dark gray—wasn't anything to write home about. Two walls were covered by paintings and photographs, all of them inartistically rendered, of groups of Sabellians, and a huge holograph of what seemed to be a very dead tree dominated one corner of the room. In fact, it dominated the *only* corner of the room, since the architect seemed to have a fondness for obtuse angles and inelegant curves. The carpet was thin and worn, made from some artifical fiber he couldn't identify, and had an irregular gray-on-gray pattern that made no sense to him at all.

Another wall was lined with books and discs, though since he couldn't read Sabellian he had no idea what subjects they covered. If the creature had a video or sound system, he hadn't spotted it yet. It also didn't have anything resembling an ashtray, although it had quickly produced a shallow hexagonal bowl for Monk's convenience—and had just as quickly opened the room's three diamond-shaped windows when it got its first whiff of his cigar.

It returned as Monk was wondering what its bathroom looked like, carrying a small transparent flask with a label pasted on one side.

"Here," it said, offering him the flask. "I hope you are feeling better."

"I will be in a minute," said Monk, trying to figure out how to open it. Finally he thought of twisting the cap in a clockwise direciton, and a moment later he was pouring a couple of ounces of alcohol into his drink. The Sabellian watched him in silent fascination.

"Thanks a heap, Batman," said Monk, stirring the concoction with a ballpoint pen and then taking a long swallow. "Ah, that's better!"

"The translating mechanism seems to have further problems with your pronunciation of my name. This time it came out as *Batman*."

"Friend, when you work for a carny, you get a carny name. From this moment forward, you're Batman."

"Is there some significance to it?"

"It came to me in a flash. You look like a bat—

that's a flying animal we've got back on Earth; ugly little beast, too, meaning no offense—and when I was a kid I used to read about a hero called Batman."

"I don't like it," said the Sabellian.

"It's that or Bruce Wayne—take your choice. Or better still, use 'em both. *That* ought to give you some variety."

The creature uttered a very audible sigh. "Batman," it said at last.

"By the way," said Monk, taking another swallow, "are you a boy or a girl—or ain't it applicable to Sabellians?"

"I am a male," responded Batman.

"Good. Then I won't feel awkward when I have to take a shower on the ship."

"You speak as if everything's settled. I have a number of questions yet to ask."

"Ask away," said Monk expansively, puffing happily on his cigar. "But before you do, let me ask you one first: why the hell do you want to be part of an animal act?"

"I don't. But I have spent my entire life on Sabellius III. I have seen sentient beings of all shapes and sizes come and go. I have heard them speak of exotic worlds and distant places, and I have always remained behind when they went to their next port of call." Batman turned his gaze out the window and looked up into the sky. "Did you not ever want to see what was beyond the next hill, what strange and unique civilizations lay beyond your own?"

"Until I got there," answered Monk. "Let me tell you up front: one world is pretty much like the next."

"I know for a fact that this is not true."

"Then Mr. Ahasuerus has been holding out on us," said Monk wryly. "Besides, we ain't exactly tourists. Whatever the worlds may look like, I guarantee that the inside of the ship and the inside of the tent don't change from one planet to the next, and that's ninety percent of what you'll be seeing."

"Nevertheless, I want the opportunity to see for myself."

"Well, far be it from me to talk you out of it," said Monk, finishing his drink and mixing another. "You'll have to forgive that little outburst of honesty; it won't happen again." He looked up at the Sabellian. "You gonna get in any trouble for walking out on your job—or, more to the point, can you get *me* in any trouble for taking you along?"

"My job, as you have doubtless noticed, consists of taking visitors to and from the spaceport. I rather suspect that the Corporation will survive without me."

"If you're so all-fired hot to see other worlds, and the Corporation hasn't got you tied up in some long-term contract, why the hell are you still here?" asked Monk.

"My work is far from demanding, and my salary is commensurate with the demands of my job. Under normal circumstances I would never manage to accumulate enough money to visit more than one or two nearby worlds. As yet, I do not even have *that* much."

"And you figure this is the cheapest way to see the galaxy?"

"That is correct," said Batman.

"Well, to business: what can you do besides talk and scare the hell out of little kids?"

"I have never seen a carnival, although I have read about them in my encyclopedia. I feel that I certainly can perform feats equal to those of an unintelligent animal."

"I sure as hell would hope so, considering that Bruno still wasn't housebroken when he died." Monk stood up, hands on hips, and studied the Sabellian with an expert eye. "Well, you look the part, I'll give you that. And as long as you got hands, I ought to be able to teach you a little juggling." He walked once around the creature. "With feet like yours, you ought to be able to walk a tightrope, too. I don't suppose you can fly or glide with those big flaps of yours?"

"No," said Batman. "They are from an earlier point in my race's evolutionary cycle."

Monk grunted and stared at him in silence for another minute. "What else can you do? Have *you* got any questions?"

Batman shrugged. "I can probably do just about anything you yourself can do—except consume alcohol, that is."

"Yeah? And what do you think *I* can do?"

"I don't know," admitted Batman. "Juggle. Jump through hoops. Walk a tightrope. Meaning no offense, but when I first saw you this morning, I would have thought even such simple tricks as those would be beyond you. It goes to show how deceiving appearances can be."

"Spare me your platitudes," said Monk dryly.

"One of the qualities of a platitude is that while it may be trite, it is self-evidently true," replied the Sabellian.

Monk chuckled. "So you might even pay to watch me perform in a ring, huh?"

"If I had the money," agreed Batman. "So would most of my friends. You really do appear quite terrifying to us, you know."

"Yeah. Well, to quote another platitude, beauty is in the eye of the—" Monk broke off suddenly. "Holy shit!" he exclaimed.

"I am afraid I am getting another incorrect translation," said Batman.

"Shut up and let me think for a minute!" said Monk excitedly. He began pacing around the room, puffing furiously on his cigar. "Goddammit, it'll work!" he announced at last.

"What will?" asked Batman, genuinely puzzled.

"What we've just been talking about!" said Monk enthusiastically.

"Platitudes?"

"Money!"

"I don't recall speaking about money." said Batman.

"Neverthegoddamnless," said Monk, "that's exactly

what we were talking about. So far Mr. Ahasuerus has been choosing nothing but humanoid worlds. We're gonna change all that!"

"I am afraid that I still don't understand you."

"You and me, we're gonna work our way back to the show, setting down on a bunch of Community worlds along the way and working on our act. On the humanoid worlds, *I'll* be the trainer and *you'll* be the animal; and on the nonhumanoid worlds, or at least on planets where you don't look too much out of place, *you'll* be the trainer and *I'll* be the animal. We'll flim-flam 'em six ways to Sunday!"

"Can *you* juggle or walk a tightrope?" asked Batman dubiously.

"Not yet I can't," admitted Monk, "but you'd be surprised what I can learn to do for money!" He finally stopped pacing long enough to turn and face the Sabellian. "Well, how does it sound to you?"

"Fine, I suppose," replied Batman. "I must confess that the less often I have to jump through hoops the better I'll like it."

"Okay," said Monk briskly. "Our next problem is language. Either you're going to have to learn mine or I'm going to have to learn yours."

"Why?"

"Because wherever we go, one or the other of us is going to be masquerading as an unintelligent animal—and unintelligent animals don't wear translators."

"Languages were never my strong suit," admitted Batman. "And, meaning no offense, yours sounds as if it would rip my throat apart just reproducing the sounds."

"Well, yours ain't exactly a piece of cake, either," replied Monk. "You know," he added, "neither of us actually has to *speak* the other's language. All we have to do is understand it. After all, animals don't talk. Now, I seem to remember Mr. Ahasuerus saying that he took a—what the hell did he call it?—a sleep-therapy course or an intensive-sleep course or something like that when he had to learn English. You got anything around here that we can rig up for that?"

"No. I've never heard of such a thing."

"Shit! Well, we'll just have to learn a dozen or so words of the other's language until we get back to the carnival and hook ourselves into the sleep machines."

"That seems fair enough," commented Batman.

"And we're gonna need some more animals."

"Why?"

"Because I've got a twenty-minute slot to fill in the specialty tent, and I never yet saw an audience that could concentrate on one thing for half that long. Also, when they see how dumb the other animals are, we'll impress 'em that much more with the main attraction."

"Will your employers approve of it?"

"Mr. Ahasuerus will think it's immoral and dishonest," said Monk with a smile. "But Thaddeus—he'll be pissed that he didn't think of it first."

"But if Mr. Ahasuerus is responsible for booking your acts . . ." began Batman.

"You ain't never been around Thaddeus Flint when he wants something," laughed Monk. "I'll guarantee he'll break Mr. Ahasuerus down inside of twenty-four hours." He paused. "Well, I suppose the next thing we gotta do is talk money. I get a piece of the specialty show's gross, against a thousand dollars a week."

"How much is that in credits?"

"I haven't got the foggiest notion," replied Monk. "But instead of putting you on salary, I think I'll give you a percent of my percent. I ain't got nothing to spend it on anyway."

"Than why are you so concerned with money?"

"Call it the capitalist ethic," said Monk. "How else am I gonna measure how well I'm doing?" He mixed up still another drink. "I think we'll split two-thirds for me, one-third for you."

"I *do* have things to spend my money on," said

Batman slowly, "and it seems that if I am to do essentially the same work as you, a fifty-fifty split would be more equitable."

"We ain't talking equitable," responded Monk. "We're talking about an unhappy red bat who's looking to get off his planet."

Batman shrugged in resignation. "Two-thirds to one-third," he agreed.

"Well, partner," said Monk, extending his hand, "it looks like we're in business." The Sabellian looked blankly at his hand. "Take it, gentle-like, with one of your paws," Monk explained. "That's the way we seal a bargain back where I come from."

Batman extended a long, wiry hand with obvious distaste. Monk took it and shook it, trying to gauge its strength and flexibility; having worked with animals all his life and aliens for the past two years, he was well past the point of feeling repugnance at the touch of another species.

"One last thing," said Batman, withdrawing his hand the instant Monk released it and wiping it on a thick, furry thigh.

"Gotta give your two weeks' notice?"

The huge Sabellian shook his head. "If I were not immediately replaceable, I would be earning enough money to travel on my own. No, I wish to pose a question to you."

"Shoot."

"I am, of course, very anxious to go, so much so that I am willing to do whatever is required of me. But doesn't deceiving your audience in this way bother you at all?"

"That's show biz," said Monk with a smile.

"You have no moral compunctions about it?" persisted Batman.

"Hell, no," replied Monk. "As Thaddeus says, if God didn't want them fleeced, He wouldn't have made 'em sheep. Words to live by, once you become a carny." Monk paused. "Why? You getting cold feet about fooling all them innocent marks?"

"No," said Batman. "But I had rather expected you to be different."

"Aside from the fact that you've got a terminal case of the uglies and I got the niftiest mustache anyone ever laid eyes on, we're a lot more alike than you think."

"Oh?"

"I'm a carny. That means I can spot a con man at fifty paces. Or a con *bat*, for that matter. Don't forget who volunteered to be an animal in the first place." Monk reached down and snuffed out his cigar in the makeshift ashtray. "Let's gather up your gear and get this show on the road."

"All right," said Batman. "By the way, I think I had better announce my intentions from your ship, just in case I have underestimated my importance to my employer."

"Now you're talking," said Monk, following him into his sleeping room, which was even more strangely structured than the rest of the apartment. "And don't forget to bring along all your spare alcohol."

"I intended to all along," replied Batman. "I am curious to experience the effects of the mixture you concocted."

"Bruce, baby," said Monk, lighting up another cigar, "I have the feeling that this is the beginning of a beautiful partnership."

4.

Monk turned his translating device on just in time to hear his introduction.

"And now, on loan from *The Ahasuerus and Flint Traveling Carnival and Sideshow*, for three nights only, *Quinbllxt's Super Circus* is proud to present Jupiter Monk, Animal Trainer Supreme!"

Monk, dressed in his fringed buckskin outfit, strode out into the center of the cage, waited for the spotlights to hit him, and bowed with a flourish. The humanoid audience—short, pudgy, and purple, but definitely anthropoid and mammalian in appearance—stamped their feet enthusiastically. (He had yet to find a world, other than Earth, where approval or encouragement was manifested by the clapping of hands.)

Monk nodded to a couple of the assistants that Quinbllxt had supplied him, and an instant later Mickey Mouse and Donald Duck—a pair of eighty-pound catlike animals he had recently purchased on Sigma Gamma IV—bounded into the ring. He cracked his whip twice to gain their attention and then spent about five minutes putting them through their rather simple routine. Their tricks were a little sloppy in places, and Mickey tended to sulk whenever he praised or petted Donald—but considering that this was only the second world they had played, and that he had picked them up only three weeks ago, they weren't doing too badly.

He went through an even briefer routine with John F. Kennedy and Richard M. Nixon, a pair of bright-green reptiles that resembled nothing more than undersized tyrannosaurs, replaced them in their cages, and then waited for the drumroll.

It didn't come, since no one on Balok VII had ever so much as seen a drum, and he silently cursed himself for allowing Mr. Ahasuerus to choose the act's tryout worlds. Still, it was too late to do anything about it, and besides, only the blue man knew where the Corporation's other shows were playing and whose arms to twist; so he stood patiently in the center of the ring and waited for the band to find some way to announce or demonstrate that he was about to present the *pièce de résistance* of his act. When he noticed that the Baloks were getting restless he shrugged and gestured to his assistants to release Batman into the cage.

The huge Sabellian, wearing a hidden mini-microphone, roared twice. The sound startled even Monk, and precipitated a few screams from the audience. Monk cracked his whip once and Batman clambered onto a stool, snarling furiously.

Monk turned off his translator. "Attack," he said in English.

Batman flashed him a smile, then roared and dove for him, barely allowing Monk to evade his teeth and claws. Monk cracked his whip again, missing the Sabellian by inches, and Batman roared and clutched his shoulder as if the whip had connected.

Monk maneuvered him back to the stool, commanded him to stay put, walked to the door, and took three balls from an assistant. A moment later, amid much snarling, Batman was juggling them.

The audience relaxed, and suddenly Batman hurled a ball at Monk and attacked again. This time Monk fended him off with his whip handle, forcing him back to the stool, and shortly thereafter had him jumping through a burning hoop.

"I ought to get a fucking Oscar for this," he muttered, setting up a taut wire between two stands and having the hissing, snarling, growling Sabellian walk across it. When Batman had reached the halfway point he hurled himself at Monk again, grabbing him and dragging him to the floor this time. Over and over they rolled as the audience screamed and Monk's assistants raced into the cage with their weapons drawn, but before any shots could be fired or lasers unleashed, Monk was back on his feet, his shirt covered with artificial blood. He cracked the whip twice more, and Batman cowered back into his crate, which was immediately taken out of the arena and back to the ship.

Monk stayed long enough to take a few bows and make a wobbly exit, clutching his chest as fake blood seeped through his fingers and across his torso.

As soon as he was outside the building he straightened up and walked rapidly to the ship, where he locked the hatch behind him and quickly released Batman from his crate.

"I think we gave 'em their money's worth tonight," he laughed, turning on his translator. "Too bad you can't attack me every performance, but sooner or later even a race as dumb as the Baloks is bound to get suspicious. Besides," he added wryly, "I've got a limited quantity of phony blood."

"Be a little careful with that whip handle next time," complained Batman. "You really hurt me tonight."

"Sorry," said Monk, pouring himself a glass of four-smelling and fouler-tasting Balokian beer and offering one to Batman, who took it and downed it in a single swallow. "I guess I'm still not used to seeing a seven-foot bat leaping at me with his mouth open."

Batman poured himself a refill. "You said something I couldn't understand tonight," he remarked at last.

"Just talking to myself."

"Please don't, at least not until I learn your language better. I thought I had forgotten a cue."

"Right," said Monk. He leaned back and put his

hands behind his head. "Jesus, this is one hell of a long way from what I had in mind when I set out to be an animal trainer."

"It's not exactly the way I thought I would be seeing the galaxy either," agreed Batman.

"Still," said Monk with a shrug, "the money is right. I'll lay on my couch and moan in agony for about fifteen or twenty hours, until old Quinbllxt decides to double my fee if I can find the strength to crawl out of my sickbed and give him two more shows now that everyone is talking about us." He chuckled at the thought.

"Will he agree to your terms?" asked Batman.

"You've got a lot to learn about carnies," replied Monk. "Not only will he agree to my terms, but he'll know I'm lying the whole time."

"Then why—"

"Because if he tells me he thinks I'm lying, I'll have to stay in bed to prove I ain't, and then *he* won't make any money off the publicity that's gonna come out of tonight's show, and *I* won't make any money, and *you* won't make any money—and while carnies got a lot of bad traits and habits, throwing money away ain't one of 'em."

"Are all members of your race this . . . ah . . . *creative*?" asked Batman, searching for an inoffensive word.

"I had a good teacher," replied Monk, lighting a cigar and pouring more beer into his half-full glass. Suddenly he stood up and restlessly began pacing around the small compartment, barely avoiding the desk and chairs that were set up in the middle of the room. "Wish someone had taught me how to get used to being cramped up in a spaceship," he added. "You know, back when I was a hunter, I could lie stock-still for hours, waiting for an animal to move into my sights. But that was out in the open air; I'm gonna go nuts if I have to spend much more time in this goddamned ship."

He kicked his empty chair, which was bolted to the

floor, cursed, flexed his foot tentatively, limped once more around the room, and finally sat down again.

"You never mentioned that you were a hunter," remarked Batman.

"It was back when I was just a kid," said Monk. "I started trapping bears in the Klondike—that's the area I grew up in—and selling their hides. Then the ecologists began passing laws, and suddenly it was a lot easier to sell a live animal than a dead one. Anyway, after a couple of years Alaska was pretty much trapped out, and I wound up in Africa—that's halfway around the world, and it's got a hell of a lot more animals, though not nearly as many as it used to—and started capturing animals for zoos. From there it was just a hop, skip, and jump to training 'em. Of course, you couldn't export animals for circuses, but I made a couple of deals with zoos I had supplied, and pretty soon I had myself a lion and a couple of leopards. Then I went back to the Klondike and came out with the ugliest-looking bear you ever saw." He stretched expansively, took a swallow of beer, made a face at the aftertaste, and clasped his hands behind his head. "I didn't have enough animals to latch on with a circus—most of 'em carry at least a dozen elephants and twice that many cats—so I started barnstorming the hick towns, putting on my act in high school gymnasiums and farm auctions and anyplace else that would have me. I made enough to feed the animals, but I sure as hell wasn't on the road to becoming a serious threat to the Rockefellers and the Vanderbilts. Anyway, I heard on the grapevine that Thaddeus was looking for a specialty act, so I packed up my animals into an old Greyhound bus I'd bought in Kansas and headed east. I didn't know exactly where he was playing, but once I reached New England I just followed all the angry fathers and husbands and when I hit the end of the trail, there he was."

"Some of your references are obscure, but I believe I understand the gist of it," said Batman.

"How about you?" asked Monk.

"I beg your pardon?"

"How did you start working with animals?"

"I really don't work with them," explained Batman. "I applied for a job with the Corporation, and since I was relatively unqualified they decided that I would prove less annoying escorting visiting businessmen around than doing anything else. I had only been transferred to our Animal Shipping Center a short time ago."

"And now you're a star," said Monk with a smile.

"I must confess that performing in public is an exhilarating experience," replied the Sabellian. "However, I would hardly call myself a star."

"Nonsense. I couldn't have done it without you."

"Nevertheless, I will not be a star until *I* am the trainer and *you* are the animal. I look forward to it with great anticipation."

"I'll just bet you do," said Monk dryly. "Can't wait to stick a whip handle in my belly, can you?"

"Only if it becomes necessary," said Batman, and Monk couldn't tell from the translated voice whether or not he was kidding. "And of course," added the Sabellian, "I shall really only be a star when I receive an equal share of the profits."

"Don't hold your breath," said Monk.

"I will prove to you that I am worth it."

"Maybe we'd better change the subject before you convince me that I've created some kind of Frankensteinian monster here," said Monk.

"Fine," shrugged Batman. "As long as you are giving some thought as to what tricks *you* will do on Maritou III next week."

"I'm working on it," said Monk irritably.

"*And* I must practice with the four other animals."

"What do you mean—*other*?"

"Perhaps I expressed myself poorly," said Batman.

"Perhaps."

"I wish," continued the Sabellian, "that we could

perform someday on my home world. Do you think there is any chance of it?"

"It's up to Mr. Ahasuerus—but it looked pretty uninteresting, so I'm sure you could talk him into it."

"I hope so. I would very much like to have my family and friends see me perform."

"What would they think if they had seen you tonight?" asked Monk.

"What would *you* think if you saw me make your father jump through a flaming hoop?" replied Batman.

"I think I like you better when you're being polite and timid," said Monk at last.

"You must never confuse the two," said Batman. "I am *always* polite. Only the thought of finally meeting Flint, after all you've told me about him, makes me timid. Still," he added thoughtfully, "I suppose that I must do so eventually, if I am to lead a romantic life such as yours."

"*You* stick your head in a goddamned lion's mouth and tell me how romantic it is," said Monk.

"But look at all the places you've been!" enthused the Sabellian.

"Each of 'em more boring than the last," said Monk wryly. "You know, I read a hell of a lot of science fiction when I was a kid. They predicted atomic power and rockets to the Moon and all that shit. They even predicted there'd be life on other worlds." He snorted contemptuously. "But not a one of 'em ever figured on it being so goddamned *grubby* up here. I mean, hell, the most interesting planet I've been to was the one where we picked up Kennedy and Nixon, and that one didn't hold a candle to Huntsville, Alabama."

"Then what are you doing out here?"

"I thought I told you."

"All I know is that Flint and Ahasuerus put together a carnival."

"Well, it was really Thaddeus' idea. Not at first, either, but later."

"I am afraid I am confused," said Batman. "Later than what?"

"I mean he didn't think of it right off."

Batman simply stared at him, bewildered.

"Look, I've told you that Earth doesn't know anything about your Community of Worlds, right?"

The Sabellian nodded.

"Well," continued Monk, "that doesn't mean your Community doesn't know about Earth enough to want to visit it." He paused. "I used to wonder why. Then I got out here." He took another puff on the cigar and chewed thoughtfully on the end of it. "Anyway, it seems that this Corporation you and Mr. Ahasuerus work for was sending tourists and sightseers to Earth, and kind of camouflaging them as members of a carny freak show so they wouldn't attract any official attention. Ahasuerus was the tour guide."

"And Flint befriended them?" asked Batman.

"Not hardly," chuckled Monk. "He *kidnapped* them."

"You're joking again."

"The hell I am. They were taking all our business away, so he put the snatch on the whole bunch. We hid out in Maine and Vermont. Coldest fucking winter I ever spent."

"But what happened?"

"I don't exactly know. I don't think anyone does, except Thaddeus and Ahasuerus, and maybe a little hunchback called Tojo. But somehow or other they buried the hatchet and formed a partnership, and the next thing I knew I had a chance to join the show and travel to the stars." He smiled ruefully. "And since I didn't know what the stars were like, I agreed. That was maybe two and a half years ago, give or take a month."

"Obviously you are fond of Flint," said Batman cautiously, "but I can't help observing that you make him sound like some kind of monster."

"I been talking about him for a month and *that's* your conclusion?" asked Monk, surprised.

"Well, as you have continually pointed out, he lies

and cheats and abuses his help—and while I am not acquainted with your custom of marriage, you have explained enough of it so that I understand his activities with married women to be totally unacceptable. And now you inform me that he kidnapped a group of tourists—so what else am I to think?"

"You left out that he hollers at Tojo twenty-four hours a day," said Monk with a smile.

"I know my concern amuses you," continued the Sabellian, "but since he is to be my employer, I think my trepidations are justified."

"Don't worry about him," said Monk.

"I must confess that I have been worrying about him almost nonstop since you first mentioned him," admitted Batman. "Have you been misleading me?"

"Oh, I'm not saying that Thaddeus can't be a real son of a bitch when the mood takes him. I'm just saying that worrying about him ain't going to change anything."

"Can you tell me further what he's like?"

"I can't think of anything I ain't already told you," said Monk. "He drinks more and smokes more and fucks more and lies more than me," he added, not without a touch of admiration. "Outside of that, he ain't such a bad guy. He used to have a real nasty streak. I don't know for sure that it's gone, but these days he's much too busy being prosperous to notice it."

"He *still* sounds ominous," said Batman dubiously.

Monk shook his head. "Not really. Everyone knows what they want out of life. The only difference between Thaddeus and the rest of us is that he went out and got it."

"But you make him sound so petty and mean and inconsistent."

"Who isn't?" replied Monk. "He ain't some comic-book hero, you know. He's just like the rest of the carnies, only maybe a little more so. In point of fact, we only got one real hero with the show, and he's crazy."

"Who would that be?"

"A kid called Billybuck Dancer." Monk paused long enough to shift his position and put his feet on the desk. "In fact," he mused, "I guess he ain't a kid anymore. Must be closing in on thirty now. Best goddamned man with a gun or knife I ever saw. There's a story going around that once, a few years back, he had a shootout with some outlaw down in Argentina or Brazil or somewhere, and they had it in a huge arena and charged admission. 'Course, I ain't saying it's true . . ."

"But why do you claim that he is insane?"

"Well, now, I never said he was *insane*. That's a big word; it sounds like doctors and straitjackets and funny farms. What I said was, he's crazy."

"My translator doesn't seem to recognize a difference," said Batman. "It keeps repeating the same word."

"Well, that's technology for you," said Monk. "How about *pixilated*?"

"Same thing."

"Shit!" He paused for a moment, thinking. "Let's just say that he takes his daydreaming real seriously. Does that come out different?"

Batman nodded.

"So much for that," commented Monk. "The sooner we get back and learn each other's languages, the better."

"We still will be unable to speak them."

"So what? If you understand English and I understand Sabellian, or whatever the hell you call it, what's the difference? In fact, it's probably better that we *don't* speak each other's languages. That way no one will be any the wiser. I don't know for sure, but I got a feeling there's a galactic equivalent to tarring and feathering a flim-flammer."

"It sounds gruesome," said Batman. "On Sabellius III, when someone has broken a minor law such as we're doing, we merely disfigure the offender's face and genitalia."

"And you find that less gruesome?" asked Monk.

"Most assuredly."

Monk stared at the Sabellian, once more aware that he was speaking to an alien and not just an odd-looking man.

"Well, enough of this shit," he said at last. "Maybe we'd better get back to considering what we're gonna do for an encore tomorrow."

"I could attack you again."

"I told you already, that's only good one time per world. How the hell much blood do you think I'm supposed to have, anyway? Besides, a good animal trainer doesn't get attacked every damned show. Once every couple of years is more like it. In point of fact, I've only been nailed once since we left Earth, and that was when I was breaking in an assistant who blew her cool."

"I have been meaning to ask you—how did your animals die?"

"Exotic animals like lions and leopards are pretty hard to keep alive even on Earth. They couldn't take all the changes, I suppose. One by one they just folded up their tents and died."

"I hope that doesn't happen to Mickey Mouse and the others," said Batman.

"I hope so, too," said Monk. He sighed. "But what the hell. If they die, they die. They're just window dressing anyway. *You're* what the marks are paying to see."

"And *you*."

"You're really hot to get in there and crack the whip at me, aren't you?" said Monk with some irritation.

"It will help assuage my unhappiness at the inequitable distribution of our profits," said the Sabellian dispassionately.

Monk glared at him and said nothing.

"I gather you are upset with me," said Batman after a long, uncomfortable silence.

"It ain't nothing that peeling your hide off with

my whip won't cure," replied Monk. "You might keep that in mind come tomorrow night."

"I am sorry if I spoke out of turn," said the Sabellian. "You are my friend and my partner, and I do not wish you to be mad at me."

He extended his hand, and Monk took it.

"Of course," he added, squeezing tightly, "to borrow from your vernacular, I don't like being fucked over, either."

Monk forced his face into a smile and squeezed back.

"I'm gonna let you in on a little secret," he grated.

"Oh?" asked Batman, his facial muscles drawn tight.

"What you like is a matter of complete indifference to me."

They remained motionless for five minutes.

"You have a firm grip," said Batman at last.

"Yours ain't all that flabby either," said Monk, staring unblinking at him.

"Shall we stop?" asked the Sabellian after another long pause.

"Makes no difference to me," said Monk, trying to ignore the throbbing in his hand.

The Sabellian stared at him for another long moment, then shrugged and withdrew his hand.

"Son of a bitch," muttered Monk, rubbing his hand vigorously.

"How is Flint's handshake?" asked Batman, trying to massage a little life back into his own hand.

Monk chuckled. "You try your little macho game with Thaddeus and he'll wait just long enough for you to concentrate on it before he kicks you in the balls. As a matter of fact, you ever pull it with me again and I'll do the same damned thing."

"You are not a man of honor," said the Sabellian gravely.

"You noticed," said Monk.

"I am disappointed in you."

"Yeah? Well, I seem to remember you agreeing to

a two-thirds to one-third split when you were still stuck on that little jerkwater planet."

"That was then. This is now," said Batman.

"You know, a man of honor just might find it pretty lonely aboard this ship," commented Monk.

The batlike Sabellian, cold and inscrutable, stared at the human for a long moment.

"Perhaps he would at that," he admitted.

5.

The next planet on their agenda was Kenocha. Monk decided that the similarity to the Wisconsin town was not limited to the name alone. The entire world seemed to be flat and uninteresting, and covered by dull brown scrubland. The nearest city to the spaceport—and the one at which they would be performing—was composed entirely of uninteresting gray block buildings, none of them reaching a height of more than three stories. The thoroughfares were in need of repair, the air smelled stale, and although there wasn't a cloud in the sky it seemed uncomfortably humid.

The inhabitants bore a closer resemblance to Batman than to Monk. They were tall, slender, fur-covered marsupials with huge staring eyes and soft leathery nostrils that seemed to be continually testing the wind, though Monk couldn't imagine what Kenocha had that was worth smelling.

The night of their opening performance he was having the last of the Balokian beer he had taken along—it still tasted terrible, but it was the only game in town, so to speak—when Batman entered his compartment, carrying a small cloth bag in one of his hands.

"Are you ready?" asked the Sabellian.

"I will be," responded Monk. "Relax. We ain't on for another half hour or so. Someone'll be by to cart us over to the show."

"You had best remove your clothing now, to make

sure there are no belt or elastic marks on your body when you enter the cage."

"What the hell are you talking about?" demanded Monk.

"Wild animals don't wear clothes."

"*This* one does!" snapped Monk. "I ain't going out naked in front of a bunch of goddamned overweight kangaroos!"

"You are being difficult," said Batman patiently. "You know you will appear with no clothing, so why are you arguing?"

"Back on my world, animal trainers used to dress their chimps up in clothing all the time."

"May I point out that we are not on your world?" said Batman. "If we are to successfully fool the public, you must remove your clothing. After all," he added, "should someone see through our little ruse, how long do you think it will take for word to spread to the other worlds we intend to visit?"

Monk glared at him for a moment, then began taking off his shirt and pants, cursing a blue streak the whole time.

"*Everything*," said Batman, indicating Monk's shorts.

"When I'm ready," growled the human.

"Shall we review the command words once more?"

"It's not necessary. I know 'em all."

"One last time just to be sure," said Batman.

Monk shrugged and nodded, and they went over the dozen or so commands the Sabellian would be using.

"Satisfied?" said Monk when they were through.

"Yes."

"What the hell have you got in that bag you brought in?"

Batman reached into the bag and pulled out a small, squirming, rodentlike animal.

"Pick up a pet?" asked Monk with a smile.

"Hardly," replied Batman.

"Then what's it for?"

"I'm getting preperformance jitters," confided the Sabellian. "I purchased this animal to calm me down."

"Well, if he ain't a pet, what are you going to do with him?" asked Monk curiously.

"Vivisect him."

"You're kidding, right?"

"I never joke," said Batman.

"You ain't cutting no animal apart in *my* ship!" said Monk, still not quite able to believe that the Sabellian wasn't pulling his leg.

Batman shrugged. "Then I shall do it outside." He turned and walked to the airlock.

"You ain't using any of my knives or tools either!" Monk hollered after him.

"Then I will use my hands," said Batman, vanishing into the humid Kenocha night, and leaving Monk to wonder once again just what made his partner tick.

He finished his beer and paced nervously around the compartment, whistling as loud as he could to drown out any screams the little animal might make. After a few minutes Batman reentered the ship to announce that a vehicle had arrived to take them to the arena where they would be performing.

"Did you kill it?" asked Monk, staring at him.

"Of course. Please remove your shorts."

Monk pulled his shorts off.

"Much better," said the Sabellian, staring at him. "You look *much* more hideous and repulsive like this." He turned to the hatch. "There is a cage waiting in the back of the vehicle. I have already supervised the loading of the four other animals. I'll crack the whip a few times, just for the driver's benefit, and urge you into the cage. The alternative would be putting a collar around your neck and attaching it to a chain, and I surmise that you would find that unacceptable."

Monk followed him to the hatch.

"You *really* killed it?"

"You told me you were once a hunter. Did you never kill an animal?"

"Never just to calm my nerves, you son of a bitch."

"I almost forgot," said Batman suddenly. "Take off your translator and leave it here."

Monk unfastened the mechanism and tossed it onto the desk, then fell into step behind the Sabellian, who waited until the driver could see them, then began manipulating Monk into the crate with his whip. Monk sat cross-legged on the floor of the crate, muttering to himself, for the brief eight-mile trip. Then he was unloaded and carried into a large building.

He and the four animals were placed on a cart and taken through a number of labyrinthian passageways, emerging at last in a brightly lit arena next to the large, circular performing cage.

A moment later he heard an amplified voice, which he assumed was the announcer but which sounded very similar to the gobbling of a turkey. Batman entered the ring, took a long bow and then a couple of extra ones, and began working with Mickey Mouse and Donald Duck, while Monk observed him with a practiced eye.

The Sabellian wasn't anywhere near as smooth and polished at his craft as Monk was, but the catlike animals were getting used to their routine, going through their paces almost by rote. He made a mental note to start teaching them a couple of new tricks so they wouldn't get too bored, but decided that it could wait until they hooked up with the carnival.

Kennedy and Nixon were feeling sluggish, probably because of the humidity, and Batman had enough presence of mind to cut their act short rather than force them to perform when they really weren't feeling like it. Then the ringmaster gobbled again, and suddenly Monk found himself facing an open door leading into the cage. Evidently he didn't walk through it fast enough, because one of Batman's local assistants prodded him with a sharp metal object.

"Fucking kangaroo!" Monk snapped, and walked into the ring while the assistant drew back in terror. Monk smiled as he concluded that his voice sounded like Kenocha's version of a savage maneater.

Batman turned to face him.

"Stool!" he shouted in Sabellian, and Monk clambered up onto the lightweight metal stool.

Batman had a trio of balls in the ring, each the size of a small grapefruit, and tossed them to Monk in quick succession.

"Juggle, then attack," he said.

"With pleasure," replied Monk with a smile.

He began juggling the balls, waited for a crowd reaction—a high-pitched hooting sound—and then threw each ball at Batman's head as hard as he could. The Sabellian ducked, startled, and Monk launched himself through the air at him.

"Vivisect a goddamned animal to calm your goddamned nerves, huh?" he yelled, pulling Batman to the floor. The Sabellian hit the ground with an audible thud and Monk, remembering the audience, then allowed himself to be driven back to the stool.

Batman was saying something to him, but he couldn't recognize any of the words they had rehearsed, and he assumed he was being subjected to a stream of the filthiest words known to Sabellius III. He smiled, formed his fingers into a claw, and took a swipe at Batman's face.

Batman cracked the whip twice and Monk straightened up quickly.

"Tumble," muttered the Sabellian.

Monk looked around him at the canvas flooring.

"Where's the mat?" he demanded.

"Tumble," repeated Batman.

"I ain't jumping down off of here without a goddamned mat!" he yelled.

The end of the whip shot out, nicking him on the shoulder and drawing blood.

"We got a lot to talk about when we get back to the ship!" snapped Monk.

He climbed down off the stool—there was no way he was going to begin his somersaults from a height of three feet with no mat to break his fall—and then began somersaulting and cartwheeling across the ring. When the audience began hooting again, he stopped, panting, and glared at Batman.

"Escape," whispered the Sabellian.

Monk smiled. He'd been waiting for this.

Suddenly he ran full force into Batman, knocking him painfully—a little *too* painfully, he hoped—onto the canvas. Then, screaming at the top of his lungs, he grabbed the bars of the cage and climbed halfway up to the open top, shaking his body as he had seen apes and monkeys do back in Earth's zoos.

When the crowd's cries of fear reached a crescendo, he heard the whip crack again, felt a sharp stab of pain as it dug into his right thigh, and allowed himself to be shepherded through the gate and back into his crate. He was being pulled out of the arena before Batman got around to taking his bows.

They loaded him and the four animals onto the ship, where he waited in darkness for almost two hours before Batman entered the airlock and released the latch on his crate.

"What the hell kept you?" demanded Monk, grabbing his translating device and holding it up to his lips.

"I had never seen a circus before," replied the Sabellian. "In case you forget, up until tonight *I* was always the one who was carted away."

"You ever let me sit in a crate for two hours again, and the next circus you watch is going to be seen through a couple of black eyes!"

Batman walked to the compact refrigerator unit and poured himself a glass of some strange-smelling fruit drink he had brought along from Sabellius III.

"I think it went very well tonight," he commented.

"I've been meaning to have a little chat with you about that," said Monk ominously.

"Oh?"

"Where the hell was my mat?"

"I thought it would look better without one."

"Nobody's paying you to think, you fucking bat!" snapped Monk. "You keep hassling me and I can always plunk you right back down on Sabellius!"

"But you won't," said Batman calmly.

"What makes you think so?"

"Because we made seventeen thousand credits tonight, and we're sold out for the next three performances. If you need money, as you assure me you do, then you need *me*."

"Maybe," Monk admitted with a shrug. "But let me tell you one thing here and now. If you *ever* cut me with that whip again, God help you the next time I get you in the ring!"

"I am still inexperienced with the whip," replied the Sabellian, as Monk snorted sarcastically. He paused and sipped his drink. "Be that as it may, I trust you noticed that I got more audience reaction tonight than you did at any prior performance."

"That's because you had a better animal to train," said Monk, opening the first-aid kit and tending to his shoulder and thigh.

"I can be more vicious and aggressive for the right amount of money," said Batman. He stared coldly into Monk's pale blue eyes. "I can also be more vicious and aggressive for the *wrong* sum of money, if you follow my meaning."

"Yeah?" said Monk, grinning harshly. "Listen to me, you ugly red bastard. I don't give a damn about what you do to small defenseless animals. If it's gonna come down to which of us can be more out-and-out vicious than the other, you're out of your league!"

The Sabellian smiled back at him.

"We shall see," he promised.

6.

Thaddeus Flint entered the mess hall, dialed a beer and a sandwich, and walked over to where Mr. Ahasuerus was sitting and sipping a cup of coffee.

"How come?" he said, pulling up a chair.

"I beg your pardon?" said the blue man, looking up.

"All the meat is artificial, right?"

"That is correct."

"Then how come it always comes out green?" said Flint. He offered his sandwich in evidence.

"It tastes the same as the meat you were used to," replied Mr. Ahasuerus. "Surely a little difference in color can't be that bothersome to you."

"If it wasn't that bothersome to me, I wouldn't be complaining about it, would I?" said Flint. "For two and a half years I've eaten everything those idiot galley robots have cooked up, but I draw the line at green meat."

"Obviously they're out of the proper dyes," said Mr. Ahasuerus. "You're a man of the galaxy now, Mr. Flint. Just close your eyes and eat it."

"I'm a man of Trenton, New Jersey," said Flint, "and from what I've seen of your galaxy, I wouldn't have it on a bet."

"I'll speak to the robots," said the blue man with a weary sigh.

"Thank you."

"Think nothing of it."

"If it works as well as the last ten times you spoke to them, I can tell you in advance I don't think a hell of a lot of it," responded Flint dryly. He paused long enough to light an artificial cigarette. "And while you're at it, tell them to make up another batch of these things."

"I do wish you'd give up smoking," said the blue man with obvious distaste. "It's a nasty habit."

"Your problem is that you don't think these things through, Mr. Ahasuerus," said Flint with an amused smile. "What would happen if I gave up drinking and smoking and then got sick? I'd be like a sinking ship with no cargo to throw overboard."

The blue man stared at him for a moment, then shrugged. "By the way," he said, changing the subject, "has Monk spoken to you?"

"I saw him when he showed up this morning with the four animals and the pterodactyl. Why?"

"He said he and his associate had something to discuss with you."

"Well, he knows where to find me," said Flint. "Must be some kind of scam, or he'd have hit you with it first."

"Have you any idea what it can be?" asked Mr. Ahasuerus.

"Whatever it is," replied Flint, "it's not going to amount to a hill of beans."

"How can you say that? Look at the success he's had with this notion of alternating as trainer and beast. He's netted almost half a million credits while working his way back to the show, and he's opened up virtually every oxygen world in the Community to us!"

"True," agreed Flint. "But Jupiter's only good for one decent idea every couple of years, and he's already had it." He stared thoughtfully at the glowing tip of his cigarette. "Five'll get you twenty that he comes up with a freak show. He's just dumb enough to think it'll work."

"I fail to see how you can be so certain that his suggestion, whatever it is, will not be viable," said the blue man gently.

"Look. You know robots and bookkeeping and playdates. I know people." Flint shrugged. "Besides, if there was a good idea staring us in the face, *I'd* have had it."

"Possibly this notion didn't originate with Monk," persisted the blue man. "Possibly it was suggested by the Sabellian."

"The guy with the wings?"

Mr. Ahasuerus nodded.

"Jesus!" snorted Flint. "He's even dumber than Monk!"

"Have you spoken to him?"

"I don't have to. Anyone who wants to tour your Community of Worlds isn't playing with a full deck—and anyone who's willing to do it from the inside of a cage makes Monk look like a goddamned genius."

"You're a very cynical man, Mr. Flint."

"That's one of the reasons you're on the road to becoming a very rich man, Mr. Ahasuerus." Flint took a long swig of his beer. "You know," he commented, holding the glass up before his face, "maybe I'd better give this stuff up after all. I think I'm beginning to like it." He shook his head, shoved the glass aside, and took a bite of his sandwich. "Well, what's new? I can't imagine going through a whole day without a crisis."

"Actually, things have been running very smoothly," replied Mr. Ahasuerus. "The only problem concerns Jason Diggs. It seems he wants to release three of his games workers and hire three new ones."

"Give him what he wants," said Flint. "After all, he and the Dancer bring in ninety percent of the money around here."

"He has not explicitly stated why he wants to terminate the workers in question, though," pointed out the blue man.

"What difference does it make? It's their job to get along with him, not the other way around."

Flint crumpled the plastic wrapper in which the sandwich had come and tossed it toward a trash atomizer across the room. It missed, and a plump alien, who resembled an oversized orange teddy bear, rose from a nearby table, shot him a reproachful look, picked up the wrapper, and disposed of it.

"That one could teach your robots a thing or two about housekeeping," remarked Flint. "Oh, well. Anything else?"

"Nothing much. Billybuck Dancer wants to know how many minutes his act will run now that Monk is back."

"Let's see," said Flint, staring blankly across the room. "Give Tojo about five minutes to warm them up. Then we'll break up Stogie's clown act; too much of it and the people start getting bored. Give him five minutes on each side of Monk's act, and give Monk twenty minutes." He focused on Mr. Ahasuerus. "Tell the Dancer he's got twenty-five minutes."

"He won't like that," commented Mr. Ahasuerus.

"This show has only got room for one prima donna, and you're looking at him."

"Oh, I didn't mean to imply that it's a matter of ego," said the blue man hastily. "It has just been my observation that the Dancer likes to shoot things. He's been performing for almost fifty minutes a show since Monk has been gone."

"Then I suggest you don't tell him that he's got to *like* it," said Flint easily. "Just tell him that he's got to *do* it."

The blue man shrugged.

"And tell Stogie that if I catch him picking pockets one more time his next job is going to be holding the Dancer's targets in his mouth."

"That will not be a problem on the next three worlds," remarked Mr. Ahasuerus, flashing his teeth in his grotesque equivalent of a grin.

"Doesn't anyone in this goddamned universe wear clothes?" muttered Flint. "All right—tell him not to pick pouches or purses or whatever the hell they use."

Mr. Ahasuerus excused himself for a moment,

wended his way through the maze of tables to the galley, and returned a moment later bearing four cups of coffee on a tray. After seating himself he removed the four cups, lined them up, poured cream in one, cream and sugar in the second, sugar alone in the third, and left the fourth one black. As Flint watched him midway between amusement and disbelief, he stirred all four cups and began taking a sip from each in turn.

"I think," remarked Flint, after his partner had repeated the procedure a third time and was starting on his fourth go-round, "that we'll have no more talk about my addictive habits this evening."

They fell to discussing the minutiae of the carnival's daily operation for the next few minutes, as they did every afternoon. Then Flint sensed a sudden tension among the other beings in the mess hall, and looked up to see Monk and Batman standing in the doorway.

"Calm down," Monk said to the room at large. "He's only a killer six nights a week plus Sunday afternoons." Most of the diners had not seen Monk since he had landed earlier in the day, but they took him at his word and returned to their meals, shooting the Sabellian an occasional curious glance.

Monk looked around the mess hall, finally spotted Flint and the blue man at their corner table, and walked over toward them, followed by Batman.

"I was hoping I'd find you here, Thaddeus," said the animal trainer. "Beats the hell out of searching for you under all them naked ladies in your bedroom."

"Well," answered Flint, "now that you've found me, grab a beer and a chair."

"No more booze," said Monk. "I'm in training now."

"Oh? For what?"

"Drop by the specialty tent tonight and see for yourself."

"I plan to," replied Flint. "Are you going to introduce me to your friend, or you just going to let us stare at each other all day?"

"Coming right up," said Monk. "Thaddeus Flint, say hello to Batman."

"Good name," said Flint approvingly. He extended his hand, which the Sabellian accepted gingerly under Monk's watchful eye.

"And this here's Mr. Ahasuerus."

"We met briefly outside," said the blue man.

"And now that that's over with," said Monk, "we want to use your sleep machine."

"I'm afraid I do not understand you," said Mr. Ahasuerus, as Monk sprawled on a chair and Batman carefully lowered himself onto another one with marked discomfort.

"You know—the machine that teaches you someone else's language while you're asleep," said Monk. "I got to learn Sabellian, and Batman needs to learn English."

"It's not quite as simple as you make it sound," replied Mr. Ahasuerus. "Otherwise you could assimilate an entire encyclopedia in a single night. If you do not have an aptitude for languages—and I must confess that you have yet to demonstrate one, Jupiter—it could take two or even three weeks to supply you with a passable knowledge of Batman's language, or he of yours."

"Then we haven't got any time to waste, have we?" grinned Monk.

"Which of you will be first?" asked the blue man.

"As long as we're playing a humanoid world here, it makes more sense for Batman to go first, I suppose," said Monk.

"Very well," replied Mr. Ahasuerus. "I can have it programmed and activated tonight."

"Sounds good to me," said Monk.

"Maybe you ought to set it up in the infirmary," said Flint.

"What are you talking about?" asked Monk.

"I'm talking about all those bruises and welts you're toting around," replied Flint. "You look like you ran into a brick wall, and then did it half a dozen more times just for good measure." He turned to the Sabellian. "You, too."

"We put on a vigorous performance," said Batman.

"Just so long as you don't put on a vigorous funeral," said Flint.

"May I respectfully submit a question?" said Batman, never taking his eyes from Flint.

"Submit away."

"I have counted some twenty-three separate and distinct sentient life forms since I arrived, including about a dozen of your own species. And every one of them either wears or at least carries a translating device except yourself—even Mr. Ahasuerus."

"I didn't hear a question," said Flint.

"I should have thought it would be obvious," replied Batman. "Why do you not wear a translator?"

"Because I'm the boss."

"Don't mind Thaddeus," said Monk with a laugh. "He's just a great big pussycat except when he's mad, which he is most of the time."

"I have another question," said the Sabellian, still staring unblinking at Flint.

"Somehow I'm not overwhelmed by surprise."

"I have been working for your organization for almost two months."

"Friday," said Flint.

"I do not understand."

"You want to know when you get paid. Payday around here is Friday."

"My translating mechanism seems not to have an analog word," said Batman.

"Par for the course. Monk'll explain it to you."

"Happy to," said Monk. "Maybe someday *you'll* explain to me how you know when it's Friday out here."

"It's Friday when we've got enough money to meet the payroll," replied Flint with a smile.

"How'd you like to hear about a way you can meet it a little easier?" asked Monk.

"I'd love to," said Flint. "But all you're going to do is tell me to start a freak show."

"How the hell did you know that?" demanded Monk.

"A shot in the dark," said Flint. He turned to the blue man. "That'll cost you twenty credits, Mr. Ahasuerus."

Mr. Ahasuerus merely sighed and turned to Monk. "Tell us about your idea, Jupiter," he said.

"Well, it's really more Batman's than mine." admitted Monk. "I was telling him about how the freak show drew back on Earth—meaning no offense, Mr. Ahasuerus—and he suggested that maybe there was a little money to be made on a freak show out here. Like, when we play a humanoid world, you and some of the weirder-looking games workers could be the freaks, and on the worlds where Batman's the trainer and I'm the animal, Thaddeus and Diggs and the rest could be freaks."

"I will, of course, accept a certain amount of compensation for this idea," put in the Sabellian.

"Of course," said Flint.

"Well, what do you think of it?" said Monk eagerly.

"I think you should stick to lion taming," said Flint. "In the first place, it means we'd have to carry twice our normal contingent of games workers. In the second place, no one's going to pay to see you in the ring if they think you're a freak instead of an animal."

"I hadn't thought of that," admitted Monk. "Well, so much for that million-dollar scheme." Suddenly he looked up. "How the hell is the Dancer going to be able to perform on a world where they think I'm a wild animal?"

"We'll see how he takes to makeup," said Flint. "If it hinders him too much, we'll probably have to kill that part of your act, unless we can get the audience to buy some fairy tale about how he was domesticated from birth but we plucked you out of the forest as a mature, harem-owning studhorse."

"We have a popular and unique act," said Batman. "To dismantle it because of a sharpshooter is unacceptable."

Flint turned to face the Sabellian.

"That sounds an awful lot as if you're telling me what I can and can't do," he said softly.

Something about his expression made Batman lower his eyes.

"Perhaps the translation was inappropriate," he said lamely. "What I am trying to say is that we will become more popular than this Billybuck Dancer, at which time it will be financially unfeasible for you to end our association."

"Wait until you outdraw him and we'll talk about it," said Flint. "And now, if you've got nothing further to say . . . "

Monk stood up immediately, and the Sabellian followed suit.

"If you will come by my office at about midnight," said Mr. Ahasuerus, "I shall have the language educator set up."

"Thank you," said Batman.

He turned to leave and almost bumped into an extremely old man, so ancient and weathered that his wrinkles stood out even through his clown's makeup.

"Stogie!" boomed Monk, throwing an arm around the clown's shoulders. "I haven't seen you since I got back! How the hell are you?"

"Getting by," said the old man. "Who's your pet?"

"Batman, say hello to Max Bloom, the best baggy-pants comic I ever saw."

"I am pleased to make your acquaintance," said Batman, staring at the strange-looking little man.

"Likewise, I'm sure," replied Stogie.

"My translating mechanism seems undecided concerning your name," continued Batman.

"Oh, it's Max Bloom, all right. But everyone calls me Stogie." He held up a huge cigar butt. "For this."

"Stogie used to work the strip show," explained

Monk, "until we found out that there wasn't any call for a strip show out here. I think I told you about that." The Sabellian nodded. "Anyway, these days he's kind of our goodwill ambassador. Pops into town to announce that we've arrived and goes into his Harpo Marx routine, and they follow him back to the show like he was the Pied Piper."

"Your references are somewhat obscure," replied Batman.

Monk shrugged. "What the hell. I'll explain it to you later."

"I apologize for what I said," said Stogie. "I thought Jupiter might have picked himself up a pet while he was away."

"Speaking of pets, Max, where's yours?" asked Monk.

The old man uttered a sharp whistle, and a moment later a miniature schnauzer barked once, bounded into the mess hall, and leaped into his arms.

"Hi, Schnoozle," said Monk, scratching the little dog behind its ears. "You seem to be taking to this a hell of a lot better than my cats did."

"He's a tough little customer," said Stogie. "Don't do that!" he added sharply to the dog, as it tried to lick his face. "This makeup'll make you sick. You know that."

"A fascinating animal," said Batman, staring intently at the schnauzer. "It is not sentient, you say?"

"It is also not yours," said Monk ominously. "Let's go."

"What is this type of animal called?" continued Batman, ignoring Monk's insistent tugging at his arm.

"A schnauzer," said Stogie. "Or, more generally, a dog."

"Are there any others with the carnival?"

"Let's go, damn it!" shouted Monk.

"Very interesting," said the Sabellian, running his hand delicately over Schnoodle's panting face. He turned and followed Monk out of the mess hall.

"What was *that* all about, do you suppose?" said Flint to the blue man.

"I have no idea," admitted Mr. Ahasuerus.

"Maybe I'll hunt Monk up later this afternoon and have him enlighten me," remarked Flint. He lit another cigarette. "That's some partner he brought back."

"Possibly he has hidden virtues."

"Possibly," said Flint grimly. "I wonder how long it'll take them to kill each other."

"What are you referring to?" asked the blue man.

"Didn't you see those marks on them? I know a goddamned whip slash when I see one."

"Do you think we should do anything about it?" asked Mr. Ahasuerus, genuinely worried.

"Yeah, I do."

"What?"

"I think we should rake in all the money we can while they're both able to work. Something tells me that this is a very temporary situation."

7.

"Hi, Jupiter. I heard you were back, so I thought I'd drop by and say hello."

Jason Oliver Diggs—known as Digger the Rigger because of a constitutional unwillingness ever to give a sucker an even break—walked up to the bars of the circular cage where Monk, shirtless in the hot afternoon sun, was putting Kennedy and Nixon through their daily training session.

"How're you doing, Rigger?" said Monk, never taking his eyes off the two reptiles.

"Not bad," replied Diggs. "We're running forty games tonight." He stared at the animals for a moment. "What the hell have you got here—Godzilla and Gorgo?"

"Not quite," laughed Monk. He gave Nixon an affectionate slap on the neck and then herded them into their crates, which he ordered a robot to move out of the sun. Then he stepped out of the cage and walked around to where Diggs was standing.

"Hot day," he remarked, picking up a towel and wiping the sweat from his face and torso.

"Hot world," answered Diggs. "Mr. Ahasuerus can sure pick 'em, can't he?"

Monk nodded. "Based on these worlds we keep playing, I can't help trying to figure what his home planet must be like."

"I've always thought it was half desert and half icecap, with no indoor plumbing," grinned Diggs. "Still, he seems to know where to go to drum up business."

"Hell, for all I know, we're standing in the garden spot of the whole damned galaxy," commented Monk. "At least, I didn't see anything better when I was out picking up animals."

"Well, you were never the most observant guy I ever met. Did you see what attacked you?"

"What are you talking about?"

"The one that gave you all those fresh scars on your back," said Diggs.

"I saw him," said Monk with an air of finality that seemed to preclude further questions on the subject.

"By the way, I bumped into your new partner a few minutes ago," said Diggs. "Damned near scared me out of a year's growth. Where did you find him?"

"Sabellius III."

"Must be an interesting place, if he's the dominant species."

"Looked just like Indianapolis," grinned Monk.

"Well, that's a change. I've been thinking that most of these backwater worlds bore a striking resemblance to the suburbs just outside of Omaha." He shrugged. "What's your friend's name?"

"Batman," said Monk, buttoning up his shirt and tucking it into his pants.

Diggs nodded. "Not bad. Besides, the only other thing that comes to mind is Mephistopheles, and that's too goddamned hard to pronounce. Still, I suppose he's a decent enough guy under that ugly-looking face of his."

"You think so?" said Monk sardonically.

"Well, he likes animals, which is a step in the right direction, unless you happen to be W.C. Fields."

"What makes you think he likes animals?"

"I heard him trying to buy Stogie's little dog. He really seemed taken with it."

"He did *what*?" demanded Monk.

"Relax, Jupiter," said Diggs. "You look like you've just swallowed a frog."

"Did Stogie sell it to him?"

"No. Nothing could make him part with that pooch."

Monk relaxed visibly.

"What's the problem, Jupiter?"

"Nothing," said Monk. "Excuse me, Rigger. I gotta go now."

He headed off toward the ship at a brisk walk, took the elevator up to Mr. Ahasuerus' office on the top deck, waited outside the door for a minute until he was able to manifest an outward appearance of calm, casually asked for the Sabellian's compartment number, and left as quickly as he could.

A moment later he was banging on Batman's door.

"Who is it?" asked the Sabellian.

"You know goddamned well who it is!" thundered Monk. "Now, are you gonna open this fucking door or am I gonna break it down?"

A moment later the door slid into the wall and Monk stepped into the room.

"I thought I told you to keep away from the goddamned dog!" screamed Monk.

"Yes, you did," said Batman calmly.

"Well?"

"You don't own me. I have every right to admire an animal if I wish, and I have every right to purchase it if I can."

"And do you have every right to rip it to pieces after you buy it?" demanded Monk.

"If I so desire," replied Batman.

"I'm telling you for the last time," said Monk ominously. "Keep away from Stogie's dog."

"And I'm telling you that you are not my master," said the Sabellian evenly.

"I'll see you in the ring!" snapped Monk.

He stalked out of the room, took the elevator down to the mess hall, found out that Stogie was preparing to go into the nearby town on his nightly goodwill mission, and hunted up the little clown as he was walking down the Midway.

"Hey, Max!" he hollered. "Wait up!"

Stogie turned to face him, curious.

"I was afraid I'd miss you!" panted Monk, running up to him.

"What's the matter, Jupiter?"

"Where's your dog?"

"Here, Schnoozle!" called Stogie. He placed two fingers to his lips and emitted a shrill whistle, and a few seconds later the little schnauzer raced up from behind one of the Skillo games.

"Keep an eye on him," said Monk, still panting.

"Why?" said Stogie, suddenly alert. "What's the matter?"

"Nothing. Just do what I say."

"Why is everyone interested in Schnoozle all of a sudden?" demanded Stogie, holding out his arms and letting the schnauzer leap into them.

"Who is *everyone*?"

"Your partner, for one."

"Who else?"

"Just before I put on my makeup, Thaddeus walked up to me and told me the same thing you just did."

Monk chuckled grimly. "Sometimes I forget just how sharp that son of a bitch can be."

"How about an answer?" persisted Stogie. "Why all this sudden interest in Schnoozle?"

"Oh, I just heard that this world's still got some wild meat-eaters," said Monk. "That's probably what Thaddeus was talking about. Keep tabs on him. And Max . . ."

"Yes?"

"Don't trust anyone to watch him for you."

"Like who?" demanded Stogie. "I'm a carny, Jupiter. I know when something's wrong, and I know when I'm being lied to. Is it your partner?"

"Let it drop, Max."

"This dog is all I've got left after seventy-three years, Jupiter. If there's something you're holding back, I think you owe it to me to tell me what it is."

"You ain't real gracious about accepting a little friendly advice, are you?" said Monk irritably. "Just do like I tell you and everything will be all right."

"Have it your way," sighed Stogie. "And thank you for your concern, Jupiter."

"It's okay, Max," said Monk, running his hand over Schnoozle's head and rubbing the insides of his ears. The schnauzer groaned blissfully, then shook his head vigorously when Monk withdrew his hand.

"You're the animal expert, Jupiter," said Stogie. "Why do dogs do that?"

"Do what?"

"Act like they're having an orgasm when you rub inside their ears, and then shake their heads like you've left a bee in there when you stop?"

"Who knows?" shrugged Monk. "Take care now." He turned to leave.

"I will, Jupiter," replied Stogie.

Monk waved to him and walked slowly back to his quarters. He took a brief nap, then rose about half an hour before show time, showered briefly, and put on his buckskins. He tucked his whip into his belt and made his way over to the specialty tent.

The place was filled with Prillians—three-legged birdlike creatures with small piercing brown eyes—and Tojo, a translating device attached to the lapel of his candy-striped jacket, was just introducing Stogie as Monk entered the tent.

The withered clown came out, dropped a batch of knives and forks in his best Harpo Marx style, took a few gentle pratfalls while he pretended to be chasing Schnoozle, and wound up his five-minute stint with an Emmett Kelly routine built around a broom and a spotlight of diminishing proportions.

Then Monk walked into the cage in the center of the tent, took a bow when Tojo signaled him that he had just been introduced—he was too far from the hunchback to hear anything but the translated words, which sounded like delicate chirping sounds—and ordered a robot to release Mickey Mouse and Donald Duck into the ring. He spent about six minutes putting them through their paces, worked Kennedy and Nixon for another three minutes, and then nodded to Tojo.

The little hunchback began speaking again, and half a minute later the tent reverberated to an authentic prerecorded drumroll. Then Batman was released into the ring.

Monk cracked his whip once, and the Sabellian hopped lightly onto a stool.

"I *told* you to leave the fucking dog alone!" Monk snarled, snaking out his whip and drawing blood from Batman's rib cage.

The Sabellian yelled something that Monk couldn't understand, but made no attempt to attack him.

Monk walked to a chest that had been set against the bars, opened it, and took out three balls. He tossed them as hard as he could at the Sabellian, who caught the first two but dropped the third.

The whip flicked out again, ripping into Batman's left shoulder.

"Get your mind off the dog and onto your work!" growled Monk.

The Sabellian picked up the third ball and began juggling them. As he did so, Monk strung a wire across the cage at a height of five feet.

He cracked the whip again, and Batman swung himself up to the wire and began walking across it. Monk snapped the whip twice more, never quite touching him with it, but startling him enough so that he had difficulty balancing.

Suddenly Monk became aware of a figure standing just on the other side of the bars.

"Why don't you just shoot him and get it over with?" said Flint dryly.

"You keep out of this, Thaddeus!"

"I'm your boss."

"Not when I'm in the ring, you ain't!"

"We'll talk about it later," said Flint. "In the meantime—duck!"

Monk instinctively lowered his head just as the Sabellian hurled himself into him. The two of them bounced off the bars and rolled over the floor. Monk got to his feet first and jammed the handle of his whip into Batman's stomach as the Sabellian was starting to rise. The alien exhaled with a whooshing sound, then rolled away and scrambled to his feet.

"We ain't done yet, you fucking savage!" grated Monk.

He drove Batman back to a stool, then signaled a robot to pass a hoop through the bars of the cage. Ordinarily he stood four feet away from the stool, but this time, after setting it ablaze, he doubled the usual distance.

Batman glared at him until he began moving the whip again, then stretched his arms above his head, bent forward, and dove through the hoop. The Sabellian brushed the flaming edge with his right leg, somersaulted as he landed, and quickly climbed onto another stool.

As the crowd applauded, Monk walked over to Batman's stool, stopped when he was five feet away, and deliberately turned his back.

"Go ahead, you bastard!" he muttered, raising his hands to acknowledge the cheers of the audience. "I'd love to see you try!"

The two of them remained motionless for the better part of a minute. Then, grinning triumphantly, Monk drove the Sabellian into his crate, bowed to the audience, and strode out of the cage.

As he walked by Tojo's stand, the hunchback reached out and grabbed his shoulder.

"They want an encore," he stammered.

"I'll just bet they do," growled Monk. He bowed to them again and left the tent.

The Sabellian, still bleeding from his wounds, was waiting for him when he reached his compartment.

"I want to apologize," he said.

"About time you came to your senses," muttered Monk.

"You misunderstand," replied Batman. "I wish to apologize for attacking you in the ring."

"It's part of the act."

"No. *Pretending* to attack you is part of the act. I tried to inflict serious physical damage upon you. It will not happen again."

"Fine," said Monk. "Now get lost."

"Certainly. And I trust that *you* will remember not to attack *me* at our next port of call." He paused, still gazing unblinking into Monk's eyes. "I look forward to it with great anticipation."

"I don't doubt it."

The Sabellian walked to the door and then turned back to Monk. "May I suggest," he added softly, "that you might want to brush up on your juggling?"

He left without another word.

8.

"I'll say this for your taste in worlds, Mr. Ahasuerus," remarked Flint as he looked through a porthole at the dead, barren surface of Thamaaliki II. "It's consistent."

"As I told you," responded the blue man patiently, "it was the closest nonhumanoid oxygen world where we could obtain a booking on such short notice."

"You'd think every world in the galaxy would be happy to host a carnival."

"Oh, they are. But between licenses and permissions and general paperwork . . ."

"I get the picture," said Flint. "Well, what do we call the people, or whatever passes for people around here—Thamaalikians?"

"I believe the dominant race is known, collectively, as the Birnn."

"Why not?" muttered Flint. "It makes about as much sense as anything else in your Community." He looked around the blue man's office, winced at the sight of his partner's latest incomprehensible painting, and put out his cigarette. "Well, I suppose we'd better get to work. Pull out a pencil and a sheet of paper and we'll start doping out what we have to do."

Mr. Ahasuerus pressed a small button on his desk.

"Well?" said Flint irritably, after half a minute had passed.

"I'm quite ready."

"Where's the paper?"

"My computer will record everything we say and

present us with a pair of readout sheets," replied the blue man.

"I don't like computers."

"So I've noticed."

"I don't understand them, and I don't trust what I don't understand. Get the paper."

"Doesn't it mean anything to you that my computer can perform eighty-seven thousand separate and distinct operations before I can write down the first word?" asked Mr. Ahasuerus.

"Yeah," replied Flint. "It means your computer can fuck things up eighty-seven thousand times faster than you can."

The blue man sighed wearily and pulled a pad of paper out of his desk.

"Ready?" asked Flint.

"Roger," said Mr. Ahasuerus, saluting him sardonically.

"You've been in here with your paintings too long," remarked Flint. "It's starting to rot your mind." He lit another cigarette. "Okay. Start by telling Julius Squeezer that he's barking at the specialty show."

"What about Tojo?"

"He stays in the ship. If any humans show up, the Birnn'll figure out that we're flim-flamming 'em. Not everyone is as stupid as your Corporation's executives, you know. Next, we've got to get Rigger to pick an alien he trusts—if he can find one—and have it supervise the games. Then we've got to tell Swede and the girls to keep inside the ship. And we'd better get to Stogie quick, before he suits up and goes into town—always assuming there *is* a town on this planet."

"And Dancer?"

"Don't worry about him."

"But he's due to perform in six hours!" protested Mr. Ahasuerus.

"Keep your shirt on. Everything's under control."

"I *am* your partner, Mr. Flint," persisted the blue man. "Surely you can tell me what you have in mind."

"You won't like it," said Flint. Then he shrugged.

"What the hell. You're going to have to see it sooner or later. You say these Birnn look kind of like over-sized brown possums, right?"

"That is correct—assuming your description of an opossum was accurate."

"It is—and that means Batman's going to look almost as strange to them as we do. And *that*, in turn, means that we don't have to make the Dancer look like Batman so much as we have to make him different from Monk."

"I concur."

"I was thinking of borrowing some of that green dye the robots have been using on my hamburgers and covering him with it, but then I figured that there's always the remote possibility that the Birnn are color-blind, or that maybe they're not bigots. So I got an even better idea." He grinned at the blue man. "Aren't you going to tell me that you're waiting on pins and needles?"

"Consider it said," replied Mr. Ahasuerus patiently.

"The whole time you and I have been talking, I've had Tojo rummaging through the gifts we give out at the game booths."

"For what?"

"A rubber mask. I remembered that we had one with three eyes and purple skin and antennae."

"It will never work."

"Why the hell not? Where would these jokers ever have seen a fright mask before? Besides, the Dancer's not going to mingle with the crowd. Nobody's going to be within fifty feet of him."

"It's too simple."

"Most good solutions are."

The blue man shrugged and jotted a notation on the paper.

"One last thing," added Flint. "Grab half a dozen of the aliens and tell them to construct a booth for us up by the lighting controls in the specialty tent. And have them put a one-way glass in it so we can watch the show but nobody can see in."

"Is that everything?" asked Mr. Ahasuerus, looking up from his note pad.

"I think so."

"Then here is your sheet of paper," he said, handing it to Flint. "And here," he added smugly, pressing another button and waiting for the readout to emerge from a slot in his desk, "is the verbatim transcription of our conversation."

Flint took the readout and glanced at it.

"Not bad for a computer," he commented. "Of course, it may get a little messy if Julius barfs at the specialty show, and the aliens may not know what kind of laces to put on our observation boot, and there probably aren't enough Catholics around for the Dancer to put on a fright mass. Still," he added, crumpling up the readout and tossing it into the trash atomizer, "it's better than I expected. These things may actually be useful someday."

He left the office as Mr. Ahasuerus, pen in hand, was meticulously going over his own copy of the readout and correcting all the typos, and took the elevator down to Monk's floor. He hunted up the appropriate compartment and knocked on the door.

"Just a second!" hollered Monk.

Flint waited silently for a few moments, and when the door finally slid open it was obvious that Monk had been sleeping.

"Got a minute?"

"Yeah. Come in, Thaddeus."

Flint entered the compartment and settled down on a recliner chair.

"Cigarette?" he offered, taking one for himself and holding another out to Monk.

"I'd better not. Gotta watch my wind these days." He rubbed his thinning hair vigorously, then sat down on the edge of his unmade bed. "What are you here for, Thaddeus?"

"I'm here to tell you that you can call it off if you want."

"What are you talking about?" demanded Monk.

"I'm talking about replacing survival of the fittest with survival of the stupidest."

"There's no way I'm gonna quit!" snapped Monk. "Did *he* put you up to this?"

Flint laughed. "He's probably more anxious to get into the ring tonight than *you* are. No, I figured I'd make one attempt at human decency, and since I know you're going to turn it down, I'll sit back and get rich with a clean conscience."

"Okay, your conscience is clean. Now what?"

"Now we wait for the show to start," said Flint. "You got any last wishes?"

"I wish we were on a humanoid world," said Monk with a disarming smile.

"The hell you do."

"What do you mean?"

"Look at your face, the way you're holding your body, everything about you," said Flint calmly. "You don't want a humanoid world at all. You want to prove that you can take anything he can dish out."

"What do you care what my reasons are?" demanded Monk. "You saw the crowds on the last world. You heard them. We got a bigger hand than the Dancer."

"The Dancer wasn't shooting anything that could shoot back," said Flint dryly. "What crowd wouldn't rather see two idiots trying to kill each other, instead of a marksman tossing coins into the air and drilling holes in them?"

"Then you admit we can outdraw him!" said Monk triumphantly.

"Jupiter, this may come as a surprise to you, but once I saw your act I never doubted that you could outdraw the Dancer."

"Then what's your problem?"

"At the rate you two are going, there's no way you're going to out*last* him."

"Then I'll go back to training animals."

"That's assuming you're still around," said Flint.

"Don't you worry none about who's gonna be around and who ain't!"

Flint shrugged. "All right. I did my best. At least the Lord and Mr. Ahasuerus ought to be off my back now." He took a long drag on his cigarette and fought back the urge to cough violently. "What was Batman going to do to Stogie's dog?"

"Nothing."

Flint cocked an eyebrow. "Honor among fools," he said dryly. "Well, just tell him that he'd better keep on doing nothing to it. I'll agree that what the two of you do to each other in the cage is your business. What happens outside the cage is *my* business."

He stood up to leave.

"You gonna talk to Batman now?" asked Monk.

"No."

"I don't want you playing no favorites, Thaddeus," continued Monk. "You made me the offer, you make it to him."

"I'm not playing favorites. I just don't see much sense telling him he can quit now that it's *his* turn to beat the shit out of *you*."

"Don't worry," said Monk. "It'll be a cakewalk."

"Cakes don't walk, Jupiter," said Flint. "They fall."

He left Monk's compartment, spent the next two hours making sure that the evening's arrangements were proceeding on schedule, satisfied himself that the Dancer could see out of his ridiculous-looking mask, and herded all the humans into the ship in midafternoon.

He played an hour's worth of gin rummy with Diggs—they never played for money, since neither was certain that he could outcheat the other—and, after eating a pair of hamburgers for dinner, walked over to the specialty tent and made himself comfortable in the newly constructed booth before the crowds began arriving.

Mr. Ahasuerus joined him shortly before nightfall, thoughtfully bringing him three canisters of semi-cold beer, and the two partners watched and waited as the tent began filling up.

"You know," said Flint, as the spectators continued to pour in, "if this keeps up we're going to need a bigger tent."

"Perhaps," said the blue man.

"Perhaps, nothing. These people are here just because of the Dancer's reputation. When the word gets out that we've got a little war going on, we're going to need five times as many seats."

Soon Julius Squeezer, the huge, green, good-natured reptilian wrestler, walked out into the center of the tent, a microphone in his hand and a translating mechanism slung around his thick, muscular neck.

"I see he's wearing a star-spangled bikini," observed Flint. "He must have raided one of the strippers' trunks."

The translated language of the Birnn sounded like a cacophony of grunts, squawks, and snorts, and Flint was unable to tell when the introduction was nearing its conclusion. After the wrestler had droned on for a couple of minutes, he touched his left elbow briefly with his right hand, and an instant later, to much hooting and arm-flapping on the part of the audience, Batman entered the cage.

Although he ordinarily wore no clothing, the Sabellian had made an outfit for himself out of gold lurex and one of Tojo's old striped jackets. Flint thought it looked rather silly, not unlike a colorful but ill-fitting set of farmer's coveralls that had been cut off just above the knees, but it did serve to remind the audience which of the performers was the animal and which was the sentient trainer.

Batman began with Kennedy and Nixon, worked them for about four minutes, and spent another six on Donald Duck and Mickey Mouse. Then, when the ring had been emptied of the animals, Monk's crate was wheeled up to the cage and buttressed up against the door.

Julius Squeezer began speaking again, the drumroll

was sent out over the sound system on cue, and a moment later Monk, totally naked, was shoved into the cage.

The Sabellian cracked the whip once, and Monk quickly jumped onto a stool.

There followed the juggling (Monk's arm was ripped open when he dropped a ball), and the matless tumbling (two lashes on Monk's back when he hesitated before hurling himself off the stool).

"He'll kill him, Mr. Flint," whispered Mr. Ahasuerus.

"Not tonight," replied Flint calmly.

"I don't know," said the blue man dubiously, as Batman began prodding Monk around the cage with the whip handle.

"I do. What's he going to do for fun if he kills him this soon?"

The Sabellian positioned Monk atop a stool, then walked over to a chest that had been placed in the ring and pulled out eight small hoops, each about two feet in diameter.

"*That's* a new one," remarked Flint, as Batman made two slightly uneven rows of four hoops apiece. Then the Sabellian accepted a long flaming torch that a robot passed through the bars, walked back to the hoops, and set each of them on fire as the drumroll sounded again.

"Shades of Vince Lombardi!" commented Flint with a wry smile on his lips.

"I don't understand," said the blue man.

"Keep watching. You will."

Batman cracked his whip again, while Monk stared at the eight flaming hoops as if he were as surprised as Flint.

"Surely he doesn't propose to make Monk run barefoot into the fire!" exclaimed Mr. Ahasuerus.

"Not into it," replied Flint. "*Inside* of it. It's an old football training exercise, but back where I come from they do it with rubber tires." He paused. "Though I wouldn't have put it past old Vince to use fire every now and then, just to keep his boys on their toes."

"You're speaking about it as if it were a game!" protested the blue man.

"No," said Flint seriously. "To the Green Bay Packers it's a game. To you and me it's a business, and a damned good business too. And to those two—who the hell knows?"

Monk had climbed down off the stool. He stood glowering at the Sabellian for a moment, then yelled something that Flint couldn't hear and raced through the hoops, picking his legs up as high as he could with each stride. He kicked the sixth and seventh hoops, bellowed a curse that Flint was sure could be heard as far away as the ship, and hobbled over to the stool.

As Monk had done on the previous world, the Sabellian now walked over to him, deliberately turned his back, and held his arms aloft in acknowledgment of the crowd's rabid cheering. He stood motionless for almost a full minute, then drove Monk into the crate, bowed deeply, and walked out of the tent.

The ovation didn't die down for almost five minutes. Then Billybuck Dancer, dressed in his sequined and fringed cowboy outfit and his rubber mask, began his performance. He was sharp, even for the Dancer, as he shot cigarettes out of aliens' mouths, hurled his knives with deadly accuracy, and blew the heads off all four kings from a deck of cards that had been thrown in the air some fifty feet away. He was rewarded with his usual applause, but the fever pitch of excitement spawned by the previous act had vanished, and the crowd silently filed out of the tent the instant that the Dancer disappeared from sight.

"Well, Mr. Ahasuerus," said Flint, feeling more and more constricted in the narrow confines of the booth but unwilling to let himself be seen until the show closed down for the night, "in their own suicidal way, Monk and the bat seem to have given us one hell of an attraction."

"How long can we let it continue?" asked the blue man, with as close to a worried frown as his browless face could approximate.

"It's a moot question. I don't think we could stop it if we wanted to . . . and we don't want to. Those two idiots are a gold mine as long as they stay healthy enough to work."

"And how long will that be?"

"Who knows?" shrugged Flint. "But you'd better get in touch with your pal Kargennian back at Corporation headquarters and tell him we need a bigger tent. A *lot* bigger," he added decisively.

"Shall I request a doctor as well?" asked Mr. Ahasuerus.

"You don't think either of them is going to admit the other can hurt him, do you?"

"No," admitted the blue man. "I suppose not."

"Maybe you'd better just request a coroner and let it go at that."

"You don't seem very distressed by all this," noted Mr. Ahasuerus reprovingly.

"I don't plan to lose any sleep over a situation I don't think I can change," answered Flint. "Let's just ride the gravy train for as long as it lasts."

The blue man stared at his partner, and considered the performance he had just witnessed, and wondered why every time he thought he was finally starting to understand his associates from Earth something like this had to happen to remind him of how truly alien they were.

9.

When the carnival hit Brakke, a humanoid world, Monk was the trainer again, and slashed Batman's right arm open to the bone during the very first performance. It required thirty-six stitches to close the wound, and Monk promptly opened it up again the next night. At the end of the five-day stay, the specialty show had grossed some 162,500 credits, an all-time record.

On Seltus VI, a nonhumanoid world, Monk broke a rib when Batman jabbed him with a whip handle, and had to miss the last two performances. Nevertheless, their gross for the four days he was able to perform was 209,800 credits, another record.

A new tent, capable of seating from four thousand to seven thousand aliens, depending on their size, arrived as the carnival touched down on the humanoid world of Boriba. Batman sustained second-degree burns on opening night but managed to perform at every show. The gross after eleven days: 776,200 credits.

Monk fractured his wrist when Batman raised the height of the stool prior to his tumbling run on Ramalii, a nonhumanoid world. The show set another record for attendance, and Monk refused all medical treatment until the carnival hit the galactic road once again.

As the huge ship reached the halfway point on its long voyage to Minot III, a world of tripodal hairless mammals, Flint wandered into the mess hall, dialed a beer, and walked over to his usual corner table, which was occupied by Tojo and Mr. Ahasuerus. The little hunchback was sketching some kind of mechanical contrivance, and explaining its finer points to the blue man.

"Building a better mousetrap?" asked Flint, pulling up a chair and studying the drawing, which looked like a cross between a tea kettle and a slot machine.

"I'm just showing Mr. Ahasuerus how to make cappuccino," stammered Tojo.

"I was thinking of programming the robots to construct a unit," added the blue man.

"It's no good without Amaretto," said Flint, "which I trust you have not been holding out on me."

"You can drink cappuccino without adding a liqueur," said Tojo.

"You can also shower with your socks on, which is just as aesthetically pleasing," replied Flint.

"I shall just drink espresso," said Mr. Ahasuerus defensively. "I have no intention of subjecting my system to alcohol."

"Then you don't need a cappuccino machine," said Flint with a smile.

"Ah, but how will I be able to add steamed milk without a machine?"

"What's so great about steamed milk?"

"It sounds thrilling," said Mr. Ahasuerus enthusiastically.

"You've been spending too much time talking to the dwarf," laughed Flint. "It's softened your brain, which was never all that hard to begin with."

"Have you come by only to insult me, or did you have some other reason?" asked Mr. Ahasuerus.

"First one, then the other. And since when did my insults ever bother you?"

"Since you started belittling my love of your national drink."

"My national drink is a vodka martini," said Flint. "What kind of lies have you been filling his head with, Tojo?"

"Mr. Flint," said the blue man, "if you don't come to the reason for your visit very soon, I shall impress you into service in the construction of our machine."

"You really mean it, don't you?" asked Flint in amusement.

"Absolutely."

"Nine out of ten doctors could really milk something like this," commented Flint. "You know caffeine is an addictive drug, don't you?"

"The same can be said about oxygen," answered Mr. Ahasuerus, flashing his teeth and looking very pleased with himself.

"My partner, the junkie," said Flint. "I hold you personally responsible for this, Tojo. You gave him his first cup of coffee back in Vermont or Maine or wherever the hell it was."

The hunchback tried to make a witty rejoinder, tripped on the words, and remained silent.

"Well, to business," said Flint. "I think it's time to split the specialty show into two tents—one for Billy the Kid and one for Ali and Frazier."

"Ali and Frazier?" inquired Mr. Ahasuerus.

"Monk and Batman," explained Tojo.

"Is there any particular reason why?" asked the blue man.

"People will always pay to see the Dancer," said Flint. "Why should we let 'em see Monk and the bat for free?"

"It never bothered you before."

"Monk couldn't draw flies at a watermelon party before. These days he's the biggest attraction we've got, so why not stagger the starting times and double our money?"

"Has the Dancer expressed any dissatisfaction with the present arrangement?"

Flint shook his head. "If there's anything that bothers him, I sure don't know what it is. It's just that back where I come from, it's bad business to pay two headliners when you've only got one audience. We can't dump one of the headliners, so we might as well create a second audience."

The blue man shrugged. "I have no objections."

"You have no objections at all, or you have no objections as long as I let you get back to work on your cappuccino machine?"

"None at all. But I would also like to get back to work on the machine."

"I think we're going to have to start rationing your coffee."

"If you keep teasing me," replied Mr. Ahasuerus, "I won't tell you about the good news I received this afternoon."

"All right—don't," said Flint.

"All right. I won't."

"What was it?"

"I had a communication from Kargennian. He was quite effusive in his praise for you, which is remarkable when one considers that you and he did not establish what could be termed a warm relationship the only time you met."

Flint grinned. "So the little son of a bitch likes me now, huh? Five'll get you twenty that he's putting together an animal-taming act just like ours."

"He did mention something to that effect."

"It'll never work. He'll never find two people as crazy as Monk and Batman."

"He also offered us a bonus based on the carnival's recent performance."

"Just what I need—more money I can't spend."

"I assumed that would be your attitude, so I took the liberty of requesting that your bonus be composed of a gift that would be acceptable to you."

"Now what the hell has Kargennian got that I could possibly want?"

"Nothing . . . yet," grinned Mr. Ahasuerus. "But when the next group of sightseers leaves Earth, Mr. Romany will be sending ten cases of Schlitz beer and twelve cartons of Parliament cigarettes with them. I estimate that, going through normal shipping channels, they will arrive here within three weeks."

"Well, I'll be damned!" exclaimed Flint happily. "I take back all the things I said about your disgusting addiction. Three weeks?"

"That is correct."

"Lord, I hadn't realized how much I missed the real stuff until you said that!" He looked at his beer, made a face, and threw the can toward the atomizer on the far side of the room. It missed, as usual, and Flint offered his partner an eloquent shrug. "Damned stuff doesn't even fly straight," he remarked disdainfully.

"I shall interpret that to mean that once your beer arrives, you will never miss the atomizer again," said the blue man caustically. He rose from the table, walked over to where the can lay on the floor, picked it up distastefully, disposed of it, and summoned a galley robot to mop up the beer that had spilled out onto the floor.

"You know," said Tojo, as Mr. Ahasuerus returned to the table, "if we can get beer and tobacco from Earth, maybe we should think about picking up a few more animals for Monk and Batman."

"They die too damned fast," said Flint. "That's how Monk wound up finding Batman in the first place." He shot a quick look at his partner. "But I'll bet someone we all know and love ordered about three tons of coffee while he was arranging for my cigarettes and beer."

"Tanzanian, Jamaican, Guatemalan, Sumatran, and Brazilian," said Mr. Ahasuerus happily.

"You forgot Honduran," remarked Flint.

"It lacks a certain potency," replied the blue man.

"As long as you discussed Mr. Romany, did anyone mention how he's doing with my old show?"

"He's making ends meet."

"That's all? I gave him a perfectly good carnival with established playdates and a trained crew and six rides, and all he's doing is making ends meet?"

"His function is not to amass a fortune, but to draw as little attention to himself and the freak show as possible," pointed out the blue man. "The more success he has, the more likely someone is to recognize the tourists for what they really are."

Flint snorted in derision. "Bullshit! I made a fortune displaying you guys and nobody ever guessed what you were."

Tojo shifted uncomfortably at the memory of that recent winter.

"It is not an episode in my life on which I care to dwell," said Mr. Ahasuerus.

"Why the hell not?" said Flint with a smile. "You got to see all of Vermont and half of Maine, didn't you? And besides, if it hadn't happened you wouldn't have met me, and if you hadn't met me you wouldn't be up here now, counting all your money and wondering how long it'll be before we have to put Monk and the bat in straitjackets."

As if on cue, Monk, looking disheveled and wild-eyed, burst into the hall.

"Thaddeus!" he bellowed. "You keep that fucking Sabellian out of the exercise room when I'm in it or I'll kill him!"

He turned on his heel and stalked back down the corridor.

Mr. Ahasuerus sighed. "I must admit that working with the carnival has been an interesting experience."

Batman, minus his translator, stopped by the doorway, growled something, and walked on.

"And getting more so all the time," added the blue man.

"Don't go feeling sorry for yourself," said Flint. "At least you aren't a goddamned tour guide any longer."

"True," admitted the blue man.

"Right," said Flint, picking up a pen and pulling Tojo's illustrations over. "Now let me show you how a cappuccino machine *really* works."

A moment later the two partners were totally absorbed in their newest project. Tojo kept an eye on the doorway, expecting a reappearance of Monk or Batman or both, but after a few minutes had passed it became obvious that neither one was going to return, and he turned his attention back to Flint's drawing, which was looking more and more like a bathtub distillery with every stroke of the pen.

10.

Thaddeus Flint was having a hell of a good time. He sat at his usual table in the mess hall, flanked by Jenny and Lori, two of his more regular bedmates, and luxuriated in the feel of the recessed filter of a Parliament in his mouth. A row of empty Schlitz cans formed an intricate pattern on the tabletop, and he popped open yet another, after first determining where to place it when he was through draining it of its contents.

Things, he reflected, had been going pretty damned well of late. They had played Minot III for nine days, during which time Batman missed two performances because of facial lacerations suffered while executing a new trick. They had also broken the house record again.

Next had been Belsegor, a huge world of tiny, snail-like beings. Monk had broken two toes and lost a tooth, but missed only one performance, and they had shattered Minot's record.

The Rigger's games were pulling in big money, Billybuck Dancer was filling his own tent at every performance, and even the rides were at least breaking even. And, much to Flint's surprise, Kargennian had personally delivered the beer and cigarettes just before the carny ship took off from Belsegor on its long voyage to Pi Beta II. Lori hadn't bitched to him about Jenny, Jenny hadn't bitched to him about Lori, and Mr. Ahasuerus hadn't bitched to him about anything. For the first time in three years, he felt reasonably content.

Diggs looked up from the next table, where he had been playing gin rummy with Tojo. "You keep drinking at this rate, Thaddeus," he remarked, "and you're going to run through every last drop of that stuff before we touch down on Pi Beta."

"It's a possibility," admitted Flint. "Of course, it would last a lot longer if I didn't have so many friends helping me drink it."

"This ain't a good year for radical ideas," said Diggs with a smile, as he took another sip of his own beer. "God, I've missed this stuff!"

"Hey, Dancer!" shouted Flint, as Monk and the Dancer entered the mess hall. "Come on over and grab a beer."

"Thank you, Thaddeus," said the Dancer, walking over to Flint's table and picking up a can. He popped it open, took a sip, and looked startled. "It tastes real!" he said at last.

"It ought to," replied Flint. "How about you, Jupiter? You want some?"

Monk shook his head.

"Well, sit down anyway," said Flint expansively. "I was just telling Jenny and Lori about how you used to capture monkeys by getting them drunk."

"Apes," replied Monk.

"What?"

"It wasn't monkeys. It was apes."

"All right—apes. Why don't you fill them in on the details?"

"Ain't nothing much to tell," said Monk.

"What are you talking about?" said Flint. "You used to bend our ears for hours with that story."

"Yeah. Well, that was a long time ago."

"I remember it," put in Diggs, leaning over from his own table. "Somewhere in Africa, wasn't it? Nyasaland or some such place."

Monk glared at Diggs for a moment, then turned to the two girls. "I had a contract to capture fifteen gibbons. I got 'em drunk. That's it."

"Loses a little something in the condensation, doesn't it?" remarked Diggs.

"Leave me alone!" snapped Monk. "I don't want your fucking beer, and I don't want your fucking company!"

He stalked off to a table at the farthest corner of the mess hall, sat down, and glared at the wall.

"What's eating him?" asked Diggs.

"Same as usual," replied the Dancer. "I don't think he and Batman are hitting it off real well."

"Boy, Dancer, you just don't believe in pulling your punches, do you?" laughed Flint.

The Dancer shrugged. "Maybe I'd better go on over and keep Jupiter company."

"Yeah," agreed Flint. "That's a pretty big wall there. It's got room for you both to stare at it."

The Dancer tipped his Stetson politely and walked over to Monk's table.

"You know," commented Flint, "there are days that the cowboy seems like a normal human being, and there are days I'd be willing to bet his IQ is low enough to freeze water."

"Well, nobody ever said gunfighters had to be smart," remarked Diggs. "Just fast."

Jenny suddenly jabbed Flint with an elbow, and he looked up as Batman entered the mess hall.

"For two guys who hate each other's guts, they sure keep coming around to the same places all the time," said Flint.

The Sabellian looked across the room, stared coldly at Monk for a moment, and then approached Flint's table.

"May I sit down?" he asked.

"Why not?" replied Flint. "Beer?"

"No," said Batman, easing himself gingerly onto a chair. "I have been meaning to speak to you for some time now."

"I wasn't aware that I was that hard to find," replied Flint easily. "Cigarette?"

"No."

"Small dog?"

The Sabellian stared at him expressionlessly for a moment, then continued: "I understand that our act has been a financial success."

"We're making ends meet," said Flint. "And of course you've given a whole generation of sadomasochistic voyeurs a reason to come to the carnival."

"You are making a profit."

"Yes." Flint pulled out another Parliament and lit it.

"A considerably greater profit than you made before I joined the show."

"You *are* going to get to the point sometime before we land on Pi Beta, aren't you?" asked Flint, blowing a thin stream of smoke in the alien's direction.

"I deserve half of the money," said Batman.

"Half of whose money?" said Flint with a smile. "Mine?"

"You know perfectly well what I mean."

"Then maybe you'd better see the guy you made your agreement with," said Flint, "and let me go back to drinking good old American beer and seducing these lovely young ladies."

"I could always go on strike," said the Sabellian.

"Well, I can't make you work if you don't want to," said Flint pleasantly. Suddenly his smile vanished. "But I can sure as hell make you wish you had."

"Are you threatening me?"

"Absolutely."

"I think you're bluffing."

"That's your privilege." Flint popped open another Schlitz. "You want to talk money, talk to Monk, and good luck to you. You want to fuck around with my show, you've got *me* to answer to."

"I take half the risk and suffer half the pain," said Batman. "It is unfair that I should not receive half the money."

"Who ever said that the world was fair?" responded Flint. "You made an agreement when Monk had something you wanted. You didn't think it was such a bad deal back then, did you?"

"It was always unfair."

"Win a few, lose a few."

"It is even more unfair that you and Mr. Ahasuerus allow this situation to continue."

"Mr. Ahasuerus and I aren't in the business of protecting incompetent bargainers. If you've got a grievance with Monk, talk to Monk."

"Monk and I no longer speak to each other," said Batman.

"That's hardly my fault, is it?"

"You will not be an intermediary?"

"Do I *look* like an errand boy?" asked Flint.

The Sabellian shrugged. "Then I will have to press home my arguments in the cage."

Flint returned his shrug. "You do what you have to do. Just make sure you don't kill the goose that laid the golden egg."

"I do not understand your reference."

"I don't imagine you do," said Flint, putting out his cigarette. "And now, if you're through making meaningless threats, I've got some serious drinking to do."

"Have the dwarf speak to Monk for me," said Batman suddenly.

Flint looked at Tojo, then back at Batman. "He's a hunchback, not a dwarf."

"But you call him a dwarf all the time."

"What I call him is *my* business," said Flint. "And he's not any more of an errand boy than I am."

The Sabellian rose and walked over to Tojo.

"Will you argue my case to Monk?" he asked.

"Leave him alone," said Flint softly.

"He can speak for himself," said Batman, laying a heavy hand on Tojo's shoulder. "Can't you?"

The little hunchback tried to stammer an answer, but no words came forth.

"Or can you?" continued Batman. "Possibly you would make a good addition to the act. Surely no one could mistake you for an intelligent being."

"You're hurting me," said Tojo, trying to twist free of the Sabellian's hand, which was digging into his neck and shoulder.

"Why should a misshapen creature like you receive more remuneration than I do?" demanded Batman, tightening his grip. "Come, little one," he continued, lifting Tojo to his feet and leading him over to where Flint was sitting. "Tell your master that he does not make your decisions for you, and that you will speak to Monk on my behalf."

Flint rose to meet them. "Feeling your oats tonight, aren't you?"

"This one will be my intermediary," said Batman. "And if he does not reach an agreement with Monk, I will—"

Suddenly Flint picked up his beer glass and tossed the contents in Batman's face. The Sabellian released his grasp on Tojo and lifted his hands to his eyes. As he did so Flint landed a heavy blow to his belly, and when Batman doubled over in pain and surprise Flint stepped back and delivered a heavy kick to his head. The tall alien fell over backward, and a moment later felt the legs of a chair digging into his stomach.

"What you and Monk do to each other in the cage is your business," said Flint with cold fury. "You mess around with me or the dwarf and you're playing in the big leagues. You understand?" The Sabellian made no reply, and Flint leaned heavily on the chair. "Understand?" he repeated.

"Yes," gasped Batman.

"You ever touch Tojo again and you're food for Stogie's dog. You got that?"

Suddenly Flint heard a sound behind him.

"Watch out, Thaddeus!" cried Diggs.

Flint ducked and pivoted, and caught a blow from Monk that had been aimed at the back of his head but landed on his shoulder.

"You keep your fucking hands off him!" roared Monk, unloading another roundhouse that Flint blocked with his forearm.

"What the hell's got into you, Jupiter?" demanded Flint, holding the chair between them.

"He's *mine*!" snarled Monk. "Nobody lays a finger on him but *me*!"

Flint hurled the chair into Monk's face, and the animal trainer staggered backward under the impact.

"I'm warning you, Jupiter," he said softly. "Keep away from me." He gave the Sabellian a quick kick in the ribs to keep him immobilized, then turned swiftly back to Monk.

"I didn't take all this shit so *you* could kill him!" yelled Monk. He looked around, picked up a beer can from a nearby table, and hurled it at Flint's head.

Suddenly a single shot rang out, and the can bounced off a wall.

"Maybe you'd better calm down, Jupiter," said the Dancer gently, twirling his pistol and tucking it back into his holster.

"You keep out of this, you fucking traitor!" bellowed Monk.

The Dancer stared at him pleasantly, standing absolutely motionless, his arms folded across his chest.

"All right," said Flint, breaking the silence. "Jupiter, get the hell out of here."

"You promise you won't touch him?" demanded Monk.

"I won't even help him to his feet," replied Flint.

"You damned well better not!" said Monk. He glared at Flint for a moment, then turned on his heel and left the mess hall.

"Thanks, Dancer," said Flint.

The Sabellian began getting up, and Flint pushed him back down roughly.

"I thought you told Monk—" began Batman.

"I lied," interrupted Flint. "It seems that you and I were having a little conversation when we were so rudely interrupted."

"I find it awkward to speak in this position."

"I'll just bet you do," said Flint. He placed a foot on the Sabellian's wing membrane, effectively pinning him to the floor. "So what we're going to do is this: I'm going to speak and you're going to listen. Nod your head if you understand."

Batman nodded his head silently.

"If you ever touch Tojo again, I'll kill you. If you ever touch Stogie's dog again, I'll kill you. If you ever touch me or Mr. Ahasuerus, I'll kill you. Do you understand me?"

Batman nodded again.

"Do you think I'm bluffing?"

The alien shook his head.

"Good," said Flint, stepping back. "Now you and Monk can go play your macho games in the cage and leave the grown-ups alone."

The Sabellian got painfully to his feet, brushed himself off slowly, and walked out of the mess hall.

"Thank you, Thaddeus," said Tojo.

"Are you all right?" asked Flint. "How's your shoulder?"

"It's fine," said the hunchback. "Why did he do it?"

"The bat? Just trying to learn the ground rules."

"I don't understand."

"He started as a phony animal, and he wound up sharing equal time as the trainer," explained Flint. "So he thought he'd push here and there and see what else gave. He wanted to see if he could get more money, or make me back down, or scare you into doing whatever he wanted. Absolutely normal."

"Then you're not mad at him?" asked Tojo in surprise.

"Of course not. Anybody's allowed to test the waters once."

"And if he tries again?"

"I'll kill him." Flint uttered the statement so casually that Tojo actually felt a shiver of fear course through him.

"I don't know that it's totally his fault," said Jenny. "After all, what he said is true—he's out there on the firing line as often as Jupiter."

"He made a deal," said Tojo. "A man should stick by his word."

"He didn't make a deal to go to war," interjected Diggs. "Monk started it."

"You're forgetting who just attacked Thaddeus," said Lori.

"Thaddeus hit him first," said Diggs. "It was Monk who went for him from behind. I'd say the goddamned alien's got a point."

"The goddamned alien would have killed Tojo if Thaddeus hadn't stepped in," protested Lori. "We ought to get rid of him."

"We're not getting rid of anyone," said Flint, returning to his seat and opening another beer. "The act brings in too much money."

"Then I hope Jupiter kills him," said Lori passionately.

"I'll lay seven to five that Batman comes out on top," said Diggs, throwing a handful of money on his own table. "Seven to five that Monk's the one to call it off, or not answer the bell."

Swede, the huge roughie who had just wandered in, walked over and covered Diggs' bet.

The argument over which of the two animal trainers was the more villainous continued unabated for another twenty minutes. As passions began running high, Flint picked up his glass and walked over to the Dancer's table.

"Fun and games night at the carnival," he said wryly.

The Dancer nodded pleasantly, but made no reply.

They sat in silence and watched the others for a few minutes. Finally Diggs snarled a curse at Lori and stalked out, and a moment later Swede and Jenny were yelling at each other.

"Got a question for you, Thaddeus," said the Dancer at last, with an amused smile on his boyish face.

"What?"

"How many more cages can you lay your hands on in a hurry?"

Flint chuckled. Then he looked back across the room and saw that even Tojo was starting to lose his temper, and suddenly he decided that it wasn't such a funny question after all.

11.

"Jesus, it's getting rougher every night!" muttered Monk. He picked up a sterile metal bowl and spat blood into it. "That son of a bitch knocked out two more teeth."

He was sitting, shirtless, on the examination table in the infirmary, as Priscilla, a former stripper who now worked the games, ministered to his wounds.

Tojo and Mr. Ahasuerus, both looking worried, were sitting opposite him on two of the chairs that lined the wall of the little room.

"It scared me, watching you tonight," offered the hunchback.

"I thought Thaddeus always sat in the booth," said Monk, wincing as Priscilla applied some antiseptic to a whip mark on his shoulder blade.

"He just watches on opening night," said Tojo.

The ship was sitting on the soft loamy soil of Pi Beta VI. The Pi Beta system was one of the few in the Community of Worlds to have two inhabited planets, and after Monk performed as the trainer before the amphibians of Pi Beta II, the roles were reversed before the sloth-type inhabitants of Pi Beta VI.

"Careful, goddamnit!" snapped Monk, as Priscilla placed a wad of cotton on his shoulder and began taping it down.

"I'm not a doctor!" she snapped. "Just shut up and hold still!"

"We could fill a whole book with all the things you're not!" snarled Monk in return. "Just get the hell out of here and leave me alone!"

Tight-lipped and flushed with rage, Priscilla walked to the door, then turned back to the animal trainer.

"I hope he kills you next time!" she shouted.

She was gone before he could offer a reply.

"*Now* will you let me send for our doctor?" asked Mr. Ahasuerus.

"I ain't letting no bright-yellow caterpillar go to work on me!" growled Monk. "I'll do it myself first."

He noticed that an old wound on his left calf had split open again, and began dabbing it with the cotton.

"Fucking trapeze!" he muttered. "I mean, hell, I never even rode on a swing when I was a kid! You just wait until the next time I get him in the cage. We'll see just how goddamned well he can run an obstacle course after I set it on fire and stick him on roller skates!"

"You and Batman are thinking, rational creatures," began Mr. Ahasuerus. "Surely—"

"Who are you calling a creature?" demanded Monk.

"Thinking, rational *beings*," amended the blue man. "Surely you can discuss the situation together. I will even volunteer to act in the capacity of a moderator or referee if that will help."

"Where'd you ever get the idea that he's a rational being?" said Monk with a bitter laugh.

"I left my world almost forty years ago," said Mr. Ahasuerus. "I left it because I was convinced that *all* sentient beings are basically decent and rational. I have seen no reason to change my opinion."

"Seems to me that you weren't so all-fired sure of that notion back on Earth," said Monk nastily.

"Mr. Flint was ultimately rational, and even humane by his own lights. Can't you see that this contest between you and Batman has gotten out of hand? There is no problem so great that it can't be reasoned out, no grievance so severe that a peaceful solution can't be arrived at in an amicable way."

"Shove it up your ass!" said Monk. "What Batman and I do in the cage is none of your business."

"But it is."

"Then collect your money and leave us alone."

"I wish that I could, but certain problems have arisen from your—what shall I call it?—your undeclared war."

"Don't you worry about it," replied Monk, limping to a cabinet and searching through it. "I'll be able to go on again tomorrow night."

"That was not what I had reference to," said Mr. Ahasuerus.

"Ah! Here it is!" Monk pulled out a spool of sterile suture thread and a needle, and began stitching up his calf, wincing each time the needle penetrated his skin. Tojo turned his eyes away, but the blue man watched him in rapt fascination. He put in five stitches, tied it off, and tossed the needle into a trash atomizer. "Good as new," he said, flexing his leg gingerly. "Maybe not as *pretty* as new, but you can't have everything."

"Where did you learn to do that?" asked Tojo.

"I peeked in when the caterpillar was stitching up Batman's wing the other night," said Monk with a tight smile, trying to ignore the blood that still oozed out through the stitches. "Figured it might come in handy sometime. Never thought I'd need it three days later, though."

"May I return to the subject?" asked the blue man.

"What subject was that?" said Monk.

"The divisions among the crew that your contest has caused."

"Divisions?" repeated Monk. "You mean someone on this ship is rooting for Batman?"

"I mean that a serious rift has been created."

"Fuck 'em!" snapped Monk. "This don't concern 'em—unless they want to get into the cage with us."

"But you are destroying the company's morale."

"Then tell 'em not to watch," said Monk. "I don't care whose side they're on as long as they leave me alone." He brought the bowl to his mouth and spat out more blood. "I'm gonna make that bastard wish he'd never been born!"

Mr. Ahasuerus closed his eyes in exasperation, then opened them and looked directly at Monk. "What if I were to make the judgment that one or the other of you was too badly injured to perform?"

"You can't do that!" roared Monk. "You heard Thaddeus—what goes on in the cage is *our* business! You keep your blue nose out of it!"

"Don't you understand that this has gotten out of control?" persisted Mr. Ahasuerus.

"You want to see something go out of control, you try to put a stop to the act!" said Monk, his whole body starting to shake with fury.

"We'll talk about it again in the future," promised Mr. Ahasuerus, leaving the room.

The instant he was alone with Tojo, Monk's entire demeanor changed, and he collapsed on the table with a sound that was halfway between a groan and a whimper.

"Are you all right, Jupiter?" asked the hunchback, getting off his chair and shuffling over to the table.

"No, I'm not all right," said Monk, his eyes closed, his whole body limp. "He hurt me tonight, Tojo. He really did." He shot a thin jet of blood out from between his teeth.

"Why didn't you say so before?" demanded Tojo, rummaging through drawers and cabinets to see if he could find anything that might prove useful in easing Monk's pain.

"In front of a fucking alien?" said Monk. "No chance!"

"Mr. Ahasuerus?" said Tojo incredulously. "He's one of us!"

"The only difference between him and Batman is that he ain't got the guts to get into the cage."

"That's not his job," stammered the hunchback.

"The cage is all there is!" shouted Monk, painfully sitting up again. "It's all that matters! Everything else is bullshit!"

"Maybe you'd better talk to Thaddeus," said Tojo.

"You tell him to come into the cage. That's the

only place I'm talking from now on!" He got dizzily to his feet. "Help me get to my room."

They made slow progress, since Tojo was none too steady on his feet even without a burly animal trainer leaning on him, but finally they got there, and the hunchback helped Monk to lower himself onto the bed.

"I'll get him next week!" he murmured, laying his head back on the pillow.

"Sure you will," said Tojo, looking around for a blanket with which to cover him.

"You think I'm kidding?" said Monk. "Go open up my trunk."

"I never said you were kidding, Jupiter."

"Open it!"

Tojo shrugged, walked to the battered army trunk with stickers from five continents pasted on it, and lifted the top.

"Down at the bottom," said Monk. "Under the snowshoes."

Tojo reached down, fumbled around for a moment, and withdrew a long, wicked-looking whip.

"Know what that is?" asked Monk, turning on his side to face the little hunchback.

"A whip."

"Not just *any* whip, you stupid dwarf!" he snapped. "It's a *sjambok*."

"Oh."

"You don't know what the hell I'm talking about, do you?" said Monk. Tojo remained silent, and he continued, "It comes from South Africa. Even the name's an Afrikaander word. Feel it."

"It's very supple."

"Guess what it's made from."

"Antelope skin?"

Monk chuckled. "First you kill a rhino. Then you cut off its cock, treat it with oils, and hang it in the sun with lead weights spinning from the bottom. Then, when you've stretched it out to twelve or thirteen feet, you treat it again, and you've got the meanest whip anyone ever saw. That thing'll go right through an elephant's hide, or the plating on an Indian rhino."

Tojo began regarding the whip as if he were holding a bomb.

"There ain't a man alive who's ever seen one of those things in action who wouldn't rather face a firing squad than a single *sjambok*."

"Why is it here?" asked the hunchback.

"Souvenir," said Monk. "Up until now, that is. Now I finally got a use for it."

"You're not going to use it on Batman!"

"Come to the cage next week and find out for yourself!" grinned Monk, wiping a thin trickle of blood from the corner of his mouth.

"You'll kill him!"

"Not right away," promised Monk.

"You know I'm going to have to tell Thaddeus about this, don't you?"

"Tell him anything you goddamned please," said Monk. "But if you try to walk out of the room with that whip, I'm gonna try it out on a fucking hunchback before I take it into the ring with me."

Tojo dropped the *sjambok* on the floor.

"I don't know what's happened to you, or why, but I don't like you anymore, Jupiter."

"I ain't here to be liked," said Monk coldly.

"What *are* you here for?"

"To go into the cage with Batman."

Tojo shook his head and left the room, and Monk, fighting back his pain, lay on his bed and tried to imagine the Sabellian's screams as the *sjambok* cut through his flesh and ripped into his bones.

And, two levels above him, Batman fondly stroked a *praque*, the torture stick of his race, and wondered if it was too soon to bring this most subtle device into the cage that dominated his every waking thought.

12.

"Excuse me, doctor," said Mr. Ahasuerus, standing in the infirmary's doorway and tapping lightly on the wall. "May I come in?"

"It's your ship," said the physician. He—or, rather, *it*—was a Bolomite from the distant planet of Neiburi II, and looked surprisingly like Monk's offhand description: an enormous yellow caterpillar. Its name was virtually unpronounceable, but Diggs had dubbed it Fuzzy-Wuzzy the day it arrived, and the sobriquet had stuck.

"Thank you," replied the blue man, entering the room and walking over to the table, where Batman lay on his belly. "That's a nasty-looking cut," he observed.

"I will survive," replied the Sabellian.

"You won't survive too many more like this one," said the doctor. "That was a new whip Monk was using, wasn't it?"

"Save your sympathy for Monk when we hit the next world," said Batman, wincing as the doctor began applying an antiseptic salve to the deep gash on the back of his left thigh.

"Do you plan to work again tomorrow night?" asked Mr. Ahasuerus.

"Of course," said Batman. "This is opening night. I have four more performances to give before we leave Alpha Gamma VI."

"That sounds all very well and good," interjected the doctor, "but there is an excellent chance that you may not be able to walk on this leg by tomorrow night."

"You're the doctor," said the Sabellian emotionlessly. "Your job is to make it possible for me to perform."

"Monk has a point," replied the doctor. "He has his own reasons for not allowing me to work on him, and they are certainly not reasons that I agree with—but when all is said and done, I know very little about human physiology." It waddled around to the front of the table and looked directly at Batman through its huge lidless eyes. "I might add that I know even less about Sabellian physiology. I do not know what medications are harmful to you, or how long before you go into shock either from the beating you are taking or my attempts to repair the damage. If you won't call this contest off, I urge you to at least send for a medic from your home planet."

"When Monk gets a doctor of his own race," replied Batman.

The doctor shrugged, a gesture which caused its entire body to shimmy from top to bottom, creating an almost hypnotic ripple throughout its finely textured yellow hair. "*You* talk to him, Mr. Ahasuerus," it said. "Maybe you'll have better luck than I'm having."

The blue man stood against a wall where Batman could see him without having to change his position.

"This really has gone on long enough," he began.

"Has Monk agreed to call it off?" asked the Sabellian.

Mr. Ahasuerus shook his head. "Jupiter is . . . well, to put it bluntly, I believe he is no longer rational."

"That is hardly my fault."

"No one is blaming you," continued the blue man. "But since it is impossible to reason with *him,* I thought perhaps I could talk a little sense to *you.* Whatever your motives may be for participating in this battle of attrition, I do not believe you are irrational."

"How comforting," remarked Batman sardonically.

"Then, since you are in possession of your senses, why can you not see that the time has come to call it off?"

"Mr. Flint made the rules, not I," said Batman

coldly. "My behavior, even my ambition, is regulated everywhere except in the cage—but within the cage, I am free to be myself, and to compete. And while I would never say it to his face, in Monk I have a worthy competitor."

"But why the cage?" persisted Mr. Ahasuerus. "Why not some other, less harmful, form of competition?"

"You simply will not understand," said the Sabellian. "The cage is a metaphor. It is an outlet for pain and rage and victory and defeat, for all those things that make up the sentient condition."

"But what of compassion, or tolerance, or even dignity?"

"What have they to do with the subject at hand?" replied Batman. "Ask Monk. He understands."

"Monk understands almost nothing these days," said Mr. Ahasuerus. "Except that he must kill you, or you him."

"He is correct. The cage is everything. The rest is—" The Sabellian suddenly uttered an involuntary grunt of pain, as the doctor began closing his wound. "Do you *really* think I will be the first to stop?" he said at last, looking up into the blue man's eyes.

"Can't you at least go back to the way the act was when you first performed it?"

The Sabellian shook his head. "Can *you* go back to a state of innocence? Once you have become an adult, you must put aside a child's naiveté. Once you enter the cage, you must follow the scenario through to its conclusion."

"What if Monk wins?" asked Mr. Ahasuerus.

"What if he does?" responded the Sabellian. "It is his nature to destroy me, just as it is mine to destroy him."

"What will you have proved by dying in your precious cage?"

"If you do not understand, there is nothing I can say that would enlighten you." He paused. "Possibly you should ask your partner."

"I have learned enough about Mr. Flint to know

that he is concerned only with winning. How you play the game means nothing to him."

"That is probably why we do not get along," said Batman, rolling over and wincing as the doctor began applying various medications to his chest. "Certain basic concepts, such as the necessity and the nobility of pain, seem completely alien to him."

"He would say that you are a sucker," continued Mr. Ahasuerus.

"What Mr. Flint thinks of me is of no importance. He will keep out of the cage; that is all that matters."

The blue man looked helplessly toward the doctor, hoping for some assistance, some added argument that might sway the Sabellian, but the yellow alien merely shook its head and shrugged again.

"I simply cannot understand you," said Mr. Ahasuerus at last. "Jupiter is half mad; at least he has an excuse for this suicidal competition. But *you*—you just don't make any sense!"

"Understand the cage, and you will understand me," replied Batman.

"The cage, the cage!" muttered Mr. Ahasuerus, "That's all I hear from either of you."

"Then Monk is not as mad as you imagine."

"I've tried my best," said the blue man with a sigh. "I think I will have to get Mr. Flint to stop it."

"He won't, you know," said the Sabellian. "As you yourself pointed out, he is interested only in results, and we are the biggest draw the carnival possesses."

"And if Monk stops?"

The Sabellian laughed, a hideous noise that startled both the blue man and the doctor. "He will never stop."

"But if he does?"

"Then the cage is mine, and I will be your animal trainer."

"Is *that* what this is all about?"

"Fool," said the Sabellian softly, shaking his head. "You will never understand."

"You refuse to moderate what goes on in the cage?"

"You can ask me that, after what I suffered tonight?" replied Batman.

"Then perhaps you will allow me to offer a scenario that is no less likely than your own," said Mr. Ahasuerus. "As you have pointed out, my partner is interested only in results, and you have given us a handsome return on our investment."

"Continue."

"Should Jupiter be unable to perform because of some crippling injury, who do you suppose would enter the ring in his place?"

The Sabellian was silent for a long moment.

"As long as he abides by the rules of the cage," he said at last.

"It has been my observation that Mr. Flint doesn't abide by any rules that stand between him and his objective," said the blue man. "You might give that some serious consideration before you go back to work."

The Sabellian stared at the ceiling in silence, his heavy brow furrowed in concentration. Finally he spoke, without emotion, without passion, without fear.

"What must be, must be. I will not be the first to quit."

The blue man sighed again and walked to the door.

"If this is the sane one," remarked the doctor, "I'd love to hear the other one address the subject."

"Just drop by his compartment," said Mr. Ahasuerus wearily. "That's his only topic of conversation these days."

"Good," said Batman. "I should hate to think his concentration was waning."

"Be quiet and hold still," said the doctor, bending over to work on his belly. "This is going to hurt."

"It is an honorable pain," said the Sabellian serenely.

"Three or four more honorable pains like this one and your guts are going to spill all over the floor of your cherished cage," said the doctor. "Can't I at least convince you to wear some sort of protection?"

"Of course," replied Batman. "If Monk wears it first."

Mr. Ahasuerus shook his head in bewilderment and left the infirmary.

13.

"Nice night," said Flint. "If you like walking through wet ovens with weights on your shoes, that is."

He and Tojo were wandering down the Midway, Flint on his nightly inspection tour, the hunchback because he had nothing better to do before the specialty show opened for business. Alpha Gamma VI was a small, hot, humid, heavy world, populated by heavyset but discernibly humanoid beings possessed of coarse brown reticulations and a tripodal stance, and Flint was careful to avoid bumping into any of them for fear that he would bounce off like a tennis ball.

"I hear that the bat got sliced up pretty bad last night," he commented, as they walked by two of the Fascination booths and a Skillo game.

"That's what Fuzzy-Wuzzy said this morning," agreed Tojo.

"Can he work tonight?"

"He says he can."

Flint shrugged and continued walking. When he came to Diggs' Three-Card Monte game he stopped, made a production of winning three hundred credits, and passed them off to one of the Rigger's shills a few feet farther on.

He pulled a handkerchief out of his pocket and began mopping the sweat from his face.

"Jesus! I don't know how the hell the Dancer can keep adjusting to these goddamned worlds."

"Everyone has to adjust to them, Thaddeus."

"Yeah, but only the Dancer has to throw his knives

at a living target. One of these days he's going to give Barbara or Priscilla an extra navel."

"He's an amazing performer," said Tojo.

"You know," said Flint, "about every third or fourth world I blow up at him for not practicing to get used to the gravity—and every time I do, he tosses a couple of rocks in the air and whips out his gun and blows them to pieces, just like in the movies. Keeps telling me that it's just like pointing your finger." He shook his head. "I wish to hell I knew where he learned to shoot like that."

"He grew up in Texas."

"He can't be thirty years old, Tojo," said Flint. "He had to have seen five hundred oil wells before he saw his first horse." He lit a cigarette from his final carton of Parliaments. "Damn! I'm going to miss these things."

"I thought you were going to give some to the robots to duplicate," said the hunchback.

Flint snorted contemptuously at the thought of the galley robots. "Their competence starts and ends with making coffee for the skeleton." He took another puff of his cigarette. "You know, I've been bitching for six months about green meat. So did you see it tonight? Purple!"

He broke off and walked over to a booth that was selling three throws at a pile of wooden bottles for two credits, took the alien working the game aside, and explained the principle of balancing the bottles more toward the middle of the bench that supported them, and of leaning far over the counter to deliver the balls to the customer so that he would be throwing from a few feet farther away.

"No wonder that son of a bitch gave out so many prizes last night," he muttered, returning to Tojo and resuming his tour. He spotted a particularly large three-legged being hovering around the wrestling ring, and warned Swede—who was barking—to take all other comers first.

"No sense in getting old Julius all tired out in his first match," he commented.

"I've had an eye on him all night, Thaddeus," replied Swede.

"No problem, then."

"Maybe you'd better have a talk with Julius," continued Swede. "He keeps taunting him."

"Maybe you'd better tell him that we don't make any money if he gets flattened," responded Flint dryly.

"He keeps saying that if Monk and Batman can do it, *he* can."

"Do *what,* for Christ's sake?" snapped Flint. "Julius! Get your ass over here!"

The huge green wrestler lumbered over to Flint and stuck his head through the ropes.

"What's up, Thaddeus?" he hissed in his sibilant reptilian voice.

"What's this shit about you trying to get that big hunk into the ring with you?" demanded Flint.

"I can take him."

"You want an even match, fine—I'll sell seats at a thousand credits a shot. In the meantime, your job is to clean up on the weaklings."

"Monk doesn't," said the wrestler defensively.

"Monk is out of his fucking mind!" snapped Flint. "You're supposed to be sane!"

"It's not fair. I want a little competition."

"Jesus! Next thing you know you'll be wanting to fight them with one hand tied behind your back."

"I've been considering it."

"You want to fight someone one-handed, fight *me*! I'm not running a fucking handicap race here!"

"All right," said Julius Squeezer.

"All right, *what*?"

"All right, I'll fight *you* with one hand tied behind my back. After I win, will you allow me to wrestle each opponent as I see fit?"

Flint sighed and shook his head sadly. "You poor

dumb bastard," he said. "All right. We might as well nip this thing in the bud."

He clambered up to the apron, took off his straw boater and his candy-striped jacket, tossed them to Tojo, and climbed into the ring.

Suddenly the crowd became attentive. None of them knew exactly who Flint was, but it was obvious that he was a member of the carnival, and the prospect of a little internecine warfare appealed to them every bit as much out here as it did inside the specialty tent.

"You're sure you want to go through with this?" said Flint, his eyes scanning the edge of the ring until he found what he was looking for.

"I wouldn't miss it for the world," grinned Julius Squeezer. He flexed his huge shoulder muscles and took a fighting stance. Flint gave ground as the wrestler approached with one arm behind his back, and ducked once as a huge green hand reached out for him.

"I'm three times your weight, Thaddeus," said the wrestler, advancing again. "You can call this off whenever you're willing to give me the same freedom in my ring that Monk has in his cage."

"Well, you're big and you're brawny," said Flint. "No one ever said you had to be smart."

He reached down to the water bucket he had spotted, picked it up, and hurled its contents into Julius Squeezer's face. The wrestler instinctively closed his eyes, and Flint slipped the bucket over his head, hooking the handle under his chin.

"Hammer!" he yelled, and Swede tossed him the hammer that was used to ring the bell.

Flint caught it and brought it down hard on the bucket, all in one motion. The noise was deafening, and the force of the blow dropped the huge wrestler to his knees. Flint hit it again with all the force he could muster, and Julius Squeezer collapsed, face down, on the canvas.

"When Sleeping Beauty wakes up, tell him that

he's still playing by the house rules," Flint told Swede. Then he climbed back down from the ring, took his hat and coat from Tojo, and continued his sojourn through the Midway as the crowd of aliens silently spread back to make a path for him.

"What would you have done if he had removed the bucket before Swede threw you the hammer?" asked Tojo.

"Run like hell, I suppose," said Flint.

"I don't believe you."

"Good for you." Suddenly Flint paused. "Shit!" he muttered, irritated. "The stupid bastard got me all sweaty. Now I'm going to have to change shirts."

"Will Julius be all right?"

Flint smiled. "By tomorrow he ought to hear what he's supposed to be hearing." He lit another cigarette. "Monk and Batman have got this whole goddamned show going crazy, you know that?"

"You could stop it," said Tojo.

"You haven't figured it out yet, have you?" said Flint.

"Figured *what* out?"

"Those two bastards are gonna fight in that cage whether they've got an audience or not. I can stop them from doing it in the tent, but as long as they're going to do it *somewhere,* why the hell shouldn't we get paid for it?" He shook his head. "I just wish I knew how to stop everyone else from choosing up sides. It's bad for morale, and it's bad for business. Look at old Julius; ordinarily he's got about as much spunk in him as a lame rabbit. Suddenly he's John Wayne and Muhammad Ali rolled into one."

"You'll think of something," said Tojo.

"I hope so. I can't keep beating the shit out of him every night." He stopped and looked at the hunchback. "Did you know I had to break up a fight between Jenny and Barbara this afternoon?"

"I'd heard that there was some kind of commotion in the mess hall."

"Yeah, I'd say there was a little commotion. Jenny

said Monk shouldn't use his new whip and Barbara threw a cup of coffee in her face. By the time they were done it looked like a college food fight." He ground his cigarette out on the dirt and immediately lit another one. "And Stogie's taken to carrying one of the Dancer's guns. Pulls it out every time Batman even looks cross-eyed at his damned dog." He sighed. "And then I check out the nightly totals, and I can't believe my eyes. This show may be going straight to hell, but we're doing it on a golden barge." He checked his wristwatch. "Oh, well, it's time for you to go to work. Showtime in ten minutes."

"Will you be watching the performance?" asked Tojo, heading off toward the specialty tent.

"I'll be along," said Flint.

He watched the little hunchback scurry off, then stopped by his quarters for a quick change of clothes. When he emerged he went directly to the specialty tent, made a large semicircle around it, and walked in through the performers' entrance. Batman's crate had already been moved to ringside, as had the four animals, and Monk and Stogie were alone in the area, sitting silently at opposite ends of a wooden bench and staring through the tent flap at the crowd that was still filing in.

"Hi, Max," said Flint. "How's it going?"

"Just fine, Thaddeus," said Stogie, stroking his schnauzer's head as the little dog sat on his lap and looked lovingly up at him. "I must have had fifteen hundred of those ugly bastards follow me and Schnoozle out from town. They seem to like my Emmett Kelly better than my Harpo Marx, so I told Tojo that I'm going to soft-peddle the wild stuff tonight."

"Fine," said Flint. He walked over and sat down next to Monk. "I've got a little problem, Jupiter," he said softly. "I wonder if you can help me with it."

"Yeah? What is it?"

"It's Julius Squeezer."

"What's the matter with him?"

"He wants to grow up to be you."

"What the hell is that supposed to mean?" snapped Monk.

"He seems to think there's something noble about letting the marks kick the shit out of him."

"Lay off, Thaddeus."

"I keep telling him he's wrong. I mean, hell, Barbara thinks you ought to use that new whip of yours in earnest and stop taking it easy on the bat."

"Leave me alone," growled Monk.

"Hey, I'm on *your* side," said Flint. "Old Fuzzy-Wuzzy looked him over last night, and he thinks the whip might not kill him for another three or four days."

"Shut up!" yelled Monk.

"Take it easy," said Flint. "Now that you guys are getting down to the nitty-gritty, I've just naturally got to side with the human, don't I? So I was thinking that what we ought to do is announce that we're doing an extra couple of shows tonight and tomorrow." He paused and smiled. "I mean, why the hell take the chance that the bat'll live through this? After all, he's the trainer on the next world."

"What the hell are you talking about?"

"I'm on *your* side, Jupiter," said Flint in softly persuasive tones. "This thing's coming to a head, so I'm just telling you that maybe you ought to give a little serious thought to killing him before we leave Alpha Gamma."

"Kill him?" repeated Monk, shaking his head vigorously as if he was disoriented.

"That's right," continued Flint. "Hell, you've got the whip. It ought to be a piece of cake." Flint stroked the handle where it stuck out of Monk's belt. "*Sjambok*—isn't that what they call it?"

Monk nodded.

"It gives a man a hell of an edge," said Flint. "I've heard that you can peel someone down to the bone with just a dozen strokes or so."

"I don't need any fucking edge!" yelled Monk, his

eyes blazing. "You think I need *this* to win? Fuck it! I'll go in there with my bare hands!"

He threw the *sjambok* on the sawdust floor and sat motionlessly, glaring at the empty cage.

Flint offered him a cigarette, which he refused, then sat in silence next to the animal tamer while Tojo began his spiel. He watched Stogie parade around the ring, warming himself by an invisible fire, allowing Schnoozle to startle him into a pair of pratfalls, and finally sweeping the spotlight into a smaller and smaller circle until it vanished.

Then Monk arose and walked into the cage, and a moment later Mickey and Donald were performing their limited repertoire of tricks.

"Friendly crowd tonight," said Stogie, returning to the bench with the little schnauzer tucked under his arm.

"Max, do me a favor, will you?" asked Flint.

"Sure thing, Thaddeus."

Flint picked up the *sjambok* and handed it to the ancient comic. "Take this thing out and burn it."

"Happy to." Stogie paused and stared at Flint for a moment. "You figure out how you're gonna burn whatever Batman comes back with?"

"I'm working on it," said Flint with a sigh.

He walked over to the flap and looked out at the cage. Monk was just finishing with Mickey and Donald, and was preparing to put Kennedy and Nixon through their paces. Flint watched them for a couple of minutes, then turned to leave just as Stogie reentered the tent.

"Ain't you gonna watch the fireworks?" asked the clown.

"Why bother?" he said sardonically. "I'm going to get half a dozen firsthand reports before I go to bed."

"Think those guys'll ever call a truce?"

"Along about the time they put refrigeration units in hell," said Flint.

He walked out into the hot, muggy night, oblivious to the impassioned and partisan screams of the crowd as Monk and Batman took up their war where they had left off the previous evening, and found himself thinking, much to his surprise, of a spaghetti Western he had seen years ago. There had been a scene in which Clint Eastwood and Lee Van Cleef had taken turns shooting each other's hats off and grinding each other's toes into the ground with the heels of their boots.

He had paid to see that film three times, and had found the scene in question both powerful and fraught with meaning. Now, for the life of him, he couldn't imagine why.

14.

Flint was dreaming of Vermont again, of strip shows and freak shows and employees who didn't look as if they had stepped out of the Late Night Creature Features movie, when he felt a bony hand gently shake him by the shoulder.

"Mr. Flint?"

He opened one eye, saw a blue refugee from some terrified child's nightmare staring at him, and shut it again.

"Mr. Flint," repeated Mr. Ahasuerus. "Aren't you uncomfortable on that couch?"

He opened his eyes again, and after focusing them on his partner for a moment, looked beyond him and saw that Tojo and Billybuck Dancer were with him.

"You woke me up just to ask me that?" he replied caustically.

"I woke you up because we have need of my office," explained the blue man patiently.

"What time is it, anyway?"

"Early afternoon. I have been looking everywhere for you. May I inquire what you were doing here?"

"What the hell does it look like I was doing?" growled Flint, sitting up and running his hands through his hair.

"This couch was not made to accommodate human beings," continued Mr. Ahasuerus. "Is there something wrong with your own bed?"

"Nothing that couldn't be solved by putting bars around it."

"I do not understand."

"Jenny and Barbara have decided not to sleep with me until I pick a side in our little war, and Lori must have buzzed my room on the intercom twenty times to tell me which side I should choose." He shrugged eloquently. "So I came up here to get a little peace and quiet." He looked at Tojo and the Dancer, then back at Mr. Ahasuerus. "What are *you* doing here? Are they finally going to teach you the manly art of poker?"

"Close the door, Tojo," said the blue man. He waited until the hunchback had done so, then continued. "We are here to discuss the situation."

"You mean Monk and the bat?"

The blue man nodded. "Strangely enough, the three of us—and yourself, of course—constitute the only members of the carnival who have not yet taken sides. Passions are aroused, tempers are flaring, and efficiency has fallen off rather drastically." He paused. "I heard about your little contretemps with Julius Squeezer last night."

"If it's past noon he ought to be okay by now," said Flint. "He was the last guy I ever thought would start feeling his oats over this thing. I thought even Billybuck here would get mad first."

"Why should I be mad?" asked the Dancer pleasantly.

"Sharing the spotlight, moving to another tent, you name it," answered Flint.

The Dancer smiled. "It don't make no difference to me, Thaddeus, as long as I get to do my act. *You're* the guy who counts the house, not me."

"A very reasonable attitude," said Mr. Ahasuerus.

"That's probably why it's so rare around here," said Flint. "As long as I'm up and awake, how about a cup of coffee?"

"Certainly," said the blue man. He walked over to a cabinet, pressed a pair of hidden buttons, and returned. "It will take about a minute."

"Fine," said Flint. "Now that you've got all us right-thinking, fair-minded people up here, what's on your mind?"

"I merely wish to explore possible courses of action without partisanship impinging upon judgment."

"Well said," smiled Flint. "And five'll get you twenty that Wyatt Earp here didn't understand one word of it."

Mr. Ahasuerus turned to explain his statement to the Dancer, and found that the trick-shot artist was staring blankly at a closet door, his mind a trillion miles and a hundred years away. Mr. Ahasuerus sighed.

"I *do* wish he could concentrate on what we have to say," the blue man said at last. "There are so few minds left that are free from this passionate advocacy that has permeated the crew."

"You start making a list of things the Dancer's mind is free of, and you just might run smack dab into Eternity," said Flint. Mr. Ahasuerus looked mildly agitated and gestured toward the marksman, and Flint waved a hand in disdain. "Don't worry about him taking offense. He doesn't see or hear anything when he's like this."

"Possibly Monk isn't the only member of the carnival who is unbalanced," suggested Mr. Ahasuerus.

"Possibly," agreed Flint. "But the Dancer's been like that ever since I've known him." He looked at the Texan's blank, pleasant face. "I'd say right now he's walking down Main Street to face Doc Holliday or Ike Clanton to protect the honor of some sweet young virgin in a gingham dress." Flint shrugged. "Why the hell shouldn't he find it more interesting than talking about a pair of animal tamers, one of 'em half crazy and the other totally weird?"

"Still . . ." began Mr. Ahasuerus.

"Don't worry about it. I'll bring him back to life when we need him. In the meantime, how's that coffee coming?"

"It should be ready now."

"I'll get it," said Tojo, clambering out of his chair and walking over to the cabinet. He opened it, found a freshly brewed pot of coffee sitting in the middle of the blue man's cherished silver serving set, poured two cups, and gave one to Flint and the other to Mr. Ahasuerus.

"Would you like anything in yours, Mr. Flint?" asked the blue man.

"Not unless you've got a shot of whiskey hidden around here," replied Flint, taking a long sip. "Is this stuff from Earth?" he asked suddenly.

"No. I ran through that some time back."

"It only arrived a few weeks ago."

"Nevertheless," replied Mr. Ahasuerus.

"So the robots made this up?"

"That is correct."

"Then why the hell can't they learn how to make a decent bottle of beer?" demanded Flint.

"We have more important things to discuss, Mr. Flint," said the blue man.

"The hell we have. Either Monk's going to kill the bat, or the bat's going to kill Monk, or they're going to kill each other, or they're both going to live. And in all four cases, I'm going to be drinking dishwater with a head on it."

"Thaddeus, maybe we really should stick to the subject," stammered Tojo.

"That's it. Take his side, you ugly little dwarf!" snapped Flint irritably. "Just forget all the things I've ever done for you and stick up for the skeleton." He finished his coffee in a single gulp. "All right. You want to know what you can do about Monk and Batman. The answer is: not a damned thing."

"I understand you managed to get Monk to relinquish his whip last night," said Mr. Ahasuerus.

"How the hell many times do you think I can do that?" said Flint. "Even Jupiter'll catch on after the ninth or tenth time—and it'll never work on Batman."

"Can we perhaps forbid either of them to use weapons or props in the ring?" asked the blue man.

"Just the lethal ones. Take 'em *all* away and I guarantee someone's going to get killed."

"But why?"

"Because when one of them's got a whip or a

prod, he knows he's got the advantage on the other—and believe it or not, neither of them really wants to destroy his meal ticket. You take that advantage away and let 'em fight on even terms and I give them three nights, tops, before one kills the other."

"You're quite sure?" asked the blue man dubiously.

"Of course I'm not quite sure!" snapped Flint. "If I knew how a madman thinks, I'd have made the Dancer a useful member of society years ago. It makes sense to *me*, but I'm not as far down the road as Monk is. Hell, for all I know, if he had his whip back tonight he'd slice the bat to ribbons."

"I spoke to Batman the night before last," continued Mr. Ahasuerus. "He is positively adamant that he will not be the first to declare a truce."

"Why should he? When either of them is the trainer, they've got no reason to quit—and when they're the animal, they won't quit until they even the score. Batman knows that all he's got to do is make it through three more nights, and then he's back in the driver's seat again."

"You make it all sound so logical," said Mr. Ahasuerus. "Until you look at the situation, and then it's not logical at all—it's madness."

"What matters isn't whether or not it's mad, but whether or not it's happening," said Flint. "And it is, and there's not a damned thing you can do about it except to fire both of them." He lit a cigarette, coughed once, and looked around for an ashtray, which the blue man quickly supplied before he could start using an *objet d'art* as a substitute. "And let me tell you something else," Flint continued. "If you stranded them here and left the cage with them, they wouldn't even know you were gone. To you and me what they're doing is business; to Diggs it's an opportunity to set up a handbook; to most of the crew it's a cause for a moral crusade—but to Monk and Batman, it's their lives. Take it away and they'd shrivel up and die."

"So you think we must let them play this out to its conclusion?"

Flint nodded his head, and the blue man turned to Tojo.

"What about you?" he asked.

"I don't know," said the hunchback. "Jupiter has been my friend since the day he joined the carnival—but he's a totally different person now. I don't know him any longer."

"Do *you* think there's any chance that he'll come to his senses?"

"He's worked with dangerous animals all his life. Every man feels fear, including Jupiter, but he's trained himself not to show it. He knows that the one thing you can't do in the ring is back down from an animal that wants to kill you. I think that, sane or crazy, he'll never back down or call it off."

"And Batman?"

"I don't know anything about him," said Tojo. "He frightens me, and I don't know why."

"Possibly because *everything* frightens you," interjected Flint sardonically.

"Possibly," said Tojo, with no trace of embarrassment. "*You* frightened me when I first met you, Mr. Ahasuerus."

"Me?" said the blue man, amused.

"Yes. When Thaddeus put you in my charge, I would have quit the show if I'd had anywhere to go. But as I got to know you, I learned how deceiving appearances can be. It's something," he said uncomfortably, "I had been telling myself every time I looked at a mirror, but it is a little harder to put in practice than you might think."

"What the hell has this got to do with the bat?" asked Flint.

"Just that the more I see of him and the more I hear him talk, the more he frightens me. Decent beings, beings like Mr. Ahasuerus and even beings like you, Thaddeus, don't have that effect on me. There's something cold about him, something cruel. Jupiter enjoys the competition and has trained himself to hide his fear—but I think Batman has no fear to hide."

He paused as he began tripping over more words than usual. "And I think he likes hurting things."

"I think you are correct," said Mr. Ahasuerus. "I do know this: he finds pain honorable."

"What do you expect from a red bat with a twenty-inch tongue?" said Flint. "He just wasn't born to be cute and cuddly."

"Then the opinion of our nonpartisan members is that one won't stop and one can't?" asked Mr. Ahasuerus.

"That's the opinion of two of us," said Flint. "Let's bring Billy the Kid back to the here and now." He picked up a pen from the blue man's desk and threw it at the Dancer, who blinked once and turned his head.

"Yes, Thaddeus?"

"What's your opinion?" said Flint.

"About what?"

"Monk and Batman."

"Jupiter could win if he'd work on his tumbling," said the Dancer serenely. "Batman never whacks him until he screws up."

"That's not what I meant," said Flint. "Are they going to stop?"

"Eventually," said the Dancer.

"Thanks a heap."

"Any time, Thaddeus," said the Dancer. He smiled politely, then turned his attention back to the closet door.

Flint looked at him for a long moment. "One of these days he's going to turn catatonic right in the ring," he said at last.

"I don't think so," said Tojo. "Put a gun or knife in his hand and he knows exactly where he is."

"Must be a hell of a comfort to his girlfriends," commented Flint dryly.

"I thought *you* monopolized all the women on this ship, Mr. Flint," remarked the blue man with a smile.

"Horseshit," said Flint irritably. "They sleep with anyone they want to. It's hardly my fault if they prefer me to crazy gunfighters and seventy-five-year-old clowns and—" Suddenly he froze, and then a huge smile spread across his face. "Hold on a second! Maybe we're missing a bet here."

"I don't follow you."

"It's been damned near a year since Jupiter has climbed into bed with anything but his pillow. That's a long time, even for a half-mad lion tamer."

"Surely you are not suggesting that the mere act of sex will bring him to his senses?" scoffed Mr. Ahasuerus.

Flint shook his head. "No, I'm not. Besides, there's no guarantee that a sane Monk would call this thing off."

"Then I am at a loss to understand what—"

"We're not talking about the *act* of sex, but the *promise* of it. I don't know how to make Monk sane, but this just might make him crazy enough to reason with. Let's see if we can't get him to want something even more than he wants to go into the cage."

"I thought you were past the point of using women like chattel," said Mr. Ahasuerus sternly.

"Chattel, hell! These aren't exactly twelve-year-old schoolgirls we're talking about. Barbara and Lori would go a quick twelve rounds in the ring for the privilege of getting Monk out of the cage before Batman kills him."

"Well," said Mr. Ahasuerus with obvious distaste, "I suppose if they're actually willing to go to bed with him . . ."

"Uh-uh," Flint corrected him. "To *promise* to go to bed with him."

"That seems flagrantly unfair, Mr. Flint," said the blue man.

"Being fair is another union," said Flint. "My job is to get one of those idiots out of the cage. And it's an unhappy fact of life, Mr. Ahasuerus, that wanting something is usually better than having it. If he actually gets one of those broads into the sack, he'll be back in the cage the next night."

"I suppose we might as well give it a try," said the

blue man unhappily. "Especially since no one else has been able to come up with an alternative."

The meeting broke up a few minutes later, and as Mr. Ahasuerus turned on his computer to enter the previous evening's totals, and the Dancer wandered aimlessly throughout the ship's corridors, Flint and Tojo took the elevator down to the mess hall.

"Do you really think it'll work, Thaddeus?" asked the little hunchback, as Flint settled down at his usual table and waited for Lori or Barbara to enter the ship.

"Probably not," said Flint. "Still, it's worth a shot."

"But—"

"Look," said Flint. "I like women a lot more than Monk does, and if one of 'em told me I had to quit running the carnival before she'd jump into the sack with me, I'd send her packing."

"But you're sane, and Monk isn't."

"I know. That's why I'm sure it won't work. That goddamned cage means a lot more to him than my show means to me."

"Then why try it at all?"

"Because I know my partner better than you do, and if I didn't come up with some kind of suggestion his next step would have been to talk with Monk himself, and Jupiter's reached the point where one alien looks pretty much like another to him."

"You think he'd have attacked him?"

"I do," said Flint. "As long as he's got an urge to maim things, let's keep it directed at the bat."

Lori walked into the mess hall just then, and Flint motioned her to join him at the table.

"Good afternoon, Thaddeus," she said coldly.

"Hi, kid," he replied. "Have a seat. I've got an interesting little proposition for you."

"Oh?"

He nodded. "But first, have you ever heard the Biblical story of Esther . . . ?"

15.

Flint was eating lunch at his usual corner table when Julius Squeezer entered the mess hall.

"Hey, Dancer!" he called softly.

"Yes, Thaddeus?" replied the Dancer from his table a few feet away.

"Wake up."

"I'm awake, Thaddeus," said the blond sharpshooter. "What's wrong?"

"Probably nothing," answered Flint.

"Oh," said the Dancer, turning back to his iced tea.

"But just in case this big green lizard isn't here to apologize, I want you to remember who signs your paycheck."

Julius Squeezer looked around the room, spotted Flint, and began lumbering over to him.

"Mr. Ahasuerus does," said the Dancer.

"Thanks a heap," grated Flint. He turned to face the huge wrestler. "Good morning, Julius. How're you feeling today?"

"Kind of silly," admitted Julius Squeezer.

"Not mad?"

"No. I had it coming."

"*That's* a relief," sighed Flint.

"I came by to tell you I was sorry," continued the wrestler. "I don't know what got into me."

"Forget it. Everyone makes mistakes."

"I still think I can beat you in a fair fight," he said, and Flint tensed slightly. "But I guess you don't fight fair, do you?"

"Not when I can help it," replied Flint.

"I do wish you had used some other method, though."

"Ears still ringing?" asked Flint with a smile.

"It's not that," said the wrestler. "Well, not entirely, anyway. I've fought maybe twenty people since you laid me out, and I think seventeen of them have gone after me with the bucket."

Flint chuckled with amusement. "Monkey see, monkey do."

"What's a monkey?"

"It would take too long to explain. Anyway," added Flint, extending his hand. "I'm glad we're friends again."

Julius Squeezer took his hand, briefly considered trying to crush it in his own, took a quick look at Flint's face, decided not to, and lumbered back out of the mess hall. Flint watched him leave, then turned back to the Dancer, who was staring dreamily at his glass.

"Thanks, Dancer," he said caustically.

"You're welcome, Thaddeus," said the Dancer politely.

"It's nice to know that my old friends are always ready to back me up."

"Happy to, Thaddeus," replied the Dancer with a pleasant smile. "Just say the word." He turned back to his glass.

Flint shook his head, dialed another beer—the Schlitz was long since gone, as were the Parliaments—and leaned back on his chair.

"May I join you, Mr. Flint?" said a familiar voice.

"Pull up a chair," said Flint, gesturing toward one.

"Thank you," replied Mr. Ahasuerus. He walked over, placed a tray containing three cups of coffee on the table, and sat down. "I didn't see you at the cargo ship this morning."

"No need," replied Flint. "Now that we're making money for the Corporation, I'm sure we got everything we asked for, and in perfect condition."

"Even the replacement part for the ice-cream machine," nodded Mr. Ahasuerus happily.

"And the Tilt-a-whirl?"

"Built exactly to your specifications," said the blue man, stirring each cup in turn, then adding cream to one and sugar to another.

"Figures."

"I am somewhat chagrined to admit that you were right all along," confided Mr. Ahasuerus. "Now that we are drawing the kind of attendance the Corporation wants, we seem to be having far less trouble getting what we request."

"What made you think that *this* Corporation was different from any other?" replied Flint. "I remember, back on Earth, when we ordered a training ring for Monk, Ringling Brothers ordered the same thing at just about the same time. They got theirs in four days; we waited seven months for ours." He paused and lit a cigarette. "How's our friend Kargennian doing with his animal-taming act?"

"As you anticipated," said Mr. Ahasuerus, exposing his teeth. "In fact, he has announced his intention of stopping by in the next few days to observe Monk and Batman in action, so that he can see what his act is lacking."

"It won't help him much," smiled Flint.

"I told him so, but he insisted."

"Maybe we ought to charge him an admission fee—like a carton of cigarettes and a pound of coffee."

"It's a tempting thought," admitted Mr. Ahasuerus. "But we must keep in mind that while you and I may own the carnival, the Corporation owns *us*."

"I'm trying not to lose any sleep over it," remarked Flint sardonically.

"Any word about Monk yet?" asked the blue man, taking a sip from each of his cups.

"That's really why you stopped by, isn't it?"

"Of course not," protested Mr. Ahasuerus. "I am always happy to speak with you, and of course I wanted to tell you that the cargo arrived and that Kargennian is coming and—"

"How many times do I have to tell you: never try to bullshit a bullshitter."

"Well, to be truthful, I *was* somewhat curious as to the results of Lori's assignation with Monk."

"Probably stayed up half the night trying to figure out who was doing what to who, you dirty old man," grinned Flint.

"I most certainly did not!" said Mr. Ahasuerus.

"By the way, while we're skirting around the subject, there's something I've been meaning to ask you for quite some time now."

"Oh?"

"What do *you* do for kicks? If there's a lady skeleton on board, you've kept her pretty well hidden for three years."

"There is no other member of my race on the ship, as you well know."

"Then how *do* you get your jollies, Mr. Ahasuerus?" persisted Flint.

"My sexual proclivities are none of your business, Mr. Flint," said the blue man austerely.

"Then you admit that you *have* sexual proclivities?"

"The subject is closed."

"Okay—but maybe I'd better tell Stogie that the bat isn't the only person he ought to protect his mutt from."

"I beg your pardon!" snapped Mr. Ahasuerus.

"Freely given," said Flint, as Lori entered the mess hall. She spotted Flint and began walking over to his table. "If you try to grab her while she's sitting here, I'm going to send you to your room."

"Mr. Flint!"

Flint laughed aloud at his partner's outraged dignity, then turned to Lori.

"Any luck?" he asked as she sat down.

"He's crazy, Thaddeus," she said, reaching over and taking his beer from him.

"We all know that. Did you manage to make him any crazier?"

She began to answer, noticed the blue man listening with rapt attention, and leaned over to whisper in Flint's ear.

"And he *still* wasn't interested?" exclaimed Flint.

"No."

"That's unbelievable!"

"Tojo told me you didn't think it would work."

"I thought you'd just give him a little come-on," said Flint. "You went above and beyond the call of duty."

"I like Jupiter," she said defensively. "I don't want to see him killed."

"None of us do, my dear," interjected Mr. Ahasuerus. "That's what this is all about."

"What did he do?" persisted Flint. "How did he react?"

"All he did was talk about Batman," she replied, still obviously upset. "It was 'I'll do this to him' and 'I'll do that to him,' and he'd rant and rave until he didn't sound like Jupiter any longer. Then I'd change the subject, and we'd talk about something else, and then something would set him off again, and he'd talk about all the things he's going to do to Batman, and how Batman can never make him show any pain in the cage." She paused for breath. "God! That goddamned cage! It's all he thinks about, Thaddeus. I think he spent more time talking about the cage than Batman, even."

"I told you: he's crazy."

"I know," sighed Lori. "Even so, he sure would have had me doubting myself if I didn't have you chasing me like a bull elephant in *musth* every night."

"Surely Mr. Flint never loses his dignity," remarked Mr. Ahasuerus in amused tones.

"You ought to see him," shot back Lori.

"Does he really scream and bellow like an elephant?" asked the blue man.

"We seem to have strayed away from the subject," interjected Flint uncomfortably. He stopped glaring at his partner and turned back to Lori. "No reaction at all? I mean, he *had* to know what you were doing."

"That's the wild part, Thaddeus," she replied, troubled. "I really don't think he did."

"He may be crazy, but he's not stupid."

"He's . . . well, *preoccupied*."

"So much for *that* bright idea," said Flint with a shrug of defeat. "It looks like we're back to square one."

"Not quite," said the blue man. "When we were at square one no one was trying to kill anyone."

"You're right," acknowledged Flint. "Well, we did our best." He turned to Lori. "More to the point, *you* did *your* best. Stop by after the show tonight and I'll do *my* best to convince you that you're not totally unattractive."

"*Is* there going to be a show tonight?" she asked sharply.

"Of course."

"You're going to let Jupiter and Batman keep pounding on each other?" persisted Lori.

"Until I can figure out a way to stop them."

"You could order them to stop."

He shook his head. "It wouldn't do any good."

"I'll see you around, Thaddeus," she said coldly, rising and walking briskly out of the room.

"Not a word, you blue skeleton!" grated Flint. He got up, got another beer from the galley, and was returning to the table when Tojo entered the room and approached him.

"Thaddeus," stammered the hunchback, "I think you'd better come with me right away."

"Should I come too?" asked Mr. Ahasuerus.

"I suppose so," said Tojo.

"You're all out of breath," remarked Flint as he fell into step behind the hunchback. "What's up?"

"I've been running."

"From who?"

"Not *from* anyone. *To* you."

He set off at a shuffling trot, down the long rows

of games and attractions, with Flint and the blue man at his heels. When he came to the training cage he stopped.

"All right," said Flint. "What's the problem?"

"Over here," said Tojo, walking to the animal crates. The two catlike creatures were up and alert, but one of the small dinosaurs lay on its side, its eyes glazed, panting heavily.

"Which one is it?" asked Flint.

"I think it's Kennedy," replied Tojo.

"What's wrong with him?"

"I don't know," said the hunchback. "I happened to be out this way because I noticed the latch on the training cage was getting loose and needed to be repaired, and as I passed by I heard him wheezing."

"How long has he been like this?"

"He was a little sluggish in the ring last night, but he was still able to perform."

"All right," said Flint. "Have a couple of robots isolate him from Nixon, just in case whatever he's got is catching."

"How about Mickey and Donald?" asked Tojo.

"I never saw a disease yet that affected animals from different worlds," replied Flint. "Still, it can't hurt to play it safe. Have each of them moved a couple hundred yards from the others, and make sure they're all protected from the sun and have plenty of water." He looked up at Mr. Ahasuerus. "They *do* drink water, don't they?"

"I really couldn't say," replied the blue man.

"Why don't you go ask your expensive computer what the hell they drink?" said Flint. "And while you're at it, see if it can tell you what makes them sick and what makes them well." He turned to Tojo. "Get a couple of robots out here and start moving them. I'm going to hunt Jupiter up and see what he knows about this."

Flint walked rapidly back to the ship, took the elevator up to Monk's floor, walked down the long corridor, and pounded noisily on the animal trainer's door.

"In a minute!" Monk shouted groggily.

"Don't give me any of that 'In a minute' crap, Jupiter!" snapped Flint. "Let me in or I'll bust the damned thing down!"

Monk, totally naked, opened the door an instant later.

"What the hell is it?" he asked, yawning.

"You've got a sick animal."

"What are you talking about?" asked Monk, starting to get dressed.

"Kennedy—or maybe it's Nixon. Anyway, it's one of the dinosaurs."

"Horseshit," muttered Monk. "They were fine last night."

"Tojo says one of them was sluggish."

"Well, what the hell does he expect from a dinosaur?" demanded Monk. "Where's my shirt?"

"Under the chair." Flint looked around the room. "Jesus, Jupiter—when's the last time you cleaned this place?"

"It's my goddamned room, isn't it?" growled Monk.

"You used to keep your bus spotless back on Earth."

"You want to talk about my animals, or do you want to talk about my room?"

"Your animals," said Flint, lighting a cigarette. "You didn't notice anything odd last night?"

"They're on right before Batman. I didn't pay any attention to them."

"Then how do you know they weren't sick?"

"*They*? I thought it was just one of 'em."

"Answer the question."

"Sick animals can't do tricks," said Monk. "If one of 'em hadn't performed, I'd know it. I don't ignore 'em *that* much."

"Has either of them been sick before?"

"Hell, no. They're as healthy as horses."

"I had Tojo give them water," said Flint. "Is that what they drink?"

Suddenly Monk froze.

"Oh, shit!" he said softly.

"What is it?"

"I forgot to feed them."

"Can an animal get that sick missing just one meal?" asked Flint skeptically.

Monk looked uncomfortable. "It's been longer than one meal, Thaddeus."

"How much longer?" demanded Flint.

Monk just stared at him, his eyes tortured.

"How long, Jupiter? Three days? A week?"

"I don't think it's been a week," said Monk softly.

"You don't *think* so?"

"I'm sure it hasn't."

"Some fucking animal tamer!" said Flint disgustedly. "Go back to bed."

"I've got to help them."

"You've helped them enough," said Flint. "Go back to plotting how you're going to kill the bat. You've done enough to the other animals."

"I didn't mean to—" began Monk.

"I knew you for seven years on Earth, and even when you and I were both starving, your animals never missed a meal," said Flint furiously. "Not once!"

"It's that goddamned Batman's fault!"

"For what—taking your mind off business?" demanded Flint.

"If it wasn't for him—"

"If it wasn't for him, you'd be doing a ten-minute spot ahead of the Dancer!" snapped Flint. "I'm not asking you to apologize, but don't lie to me either!"

"Thaddeus, so help me God, I didn't mean to—"

"*Shut up!*" bellowed Flint.

"What can I do?"

"Leave me alone so I can save your fucking animals!" said Flint, stalking out of the room. As he walked down the corridor to the elevator he heard Monk cursing and describing to himself all the things he planned to do to the Sabellian that evening.

Flint walked back to Kennedy's cage, found Tojo

there, and explained the situation to him. As the little hunchback hurried off to get food for the animals, Flint returned to the ship and went up to his partner's office.

"They *do* drink water," said Mr. Ahasuerus, looking up from his computer as Flint walked in the door. "I was just coming to tell you."

"They also eat food," said Flint grimly, as he sat down on one of the less uncomfortable chairs across from the blue man's desk.

"Of course they do."

"You say it as if everyone knows it."

"You don't mean to tell me that Monk forgot—"

"—to feed them. Right," said Flint. "Another day or two and I'd have had to have Dancer put a bullet into the sick one." He chuckled mirthlessly. "That'd be one for the books: a Texan shooting John F. Kennedy on some dirtball fifty thousand light-years from Dallas." He looked up sharply. "When is Kargennian due here?"

"In two or three days, I suppose," replied Mr. Ahasuerus. "Certainly within a week."

"Tell him that we've got four animals for his circus on Canphor VII."

"You're quite sure?"

"Why the hell should *they* die because Monk's too far gone to take care of them and Batman's too strange to give a damn?"

"But what will become of the act?" asked Mr. Ahasuerus.

"The audience will see what it's paying to see, without having to sit through the preliminaries."

"And if the contest should end?"

"There's only one way this contest is going to end, Mr. Ahasuerus."

"The survivor will have no animals left," the blue man pointed out.

Flint stared across the desk at his partner.

"We'll bury the survivor on the left, so tourists and sightseers will know which was which."

16.

"Good evening, Mr. Flint," said the small, rotund, red-skinned Corporation executive as Flint entered Mr. Ahasuerus' office. "It has been a long time."

"How're you doing, hotshot?" replied Flint, searching for an ashtray. Finally he found one, picked it up, and walked to a couch.

"I do wish you would call me by my name," said Kargennian, his colorful metallic robe glittering brightly as he shifted his position.

"Look," said Flint. "I don't like you and you don't like me. As long as we make money for you, we'll get along no matter what I call you, and when we stop making money, calling you Kargennian isn't going to keep my head off the chopping block."

"We could at least cultivate the illusion of friendship," persisted Kargennian.

"I like things fine just the way they are," replied Flint. He turned to the blue man. "Have you told him about the animals yet?"

"Yes," said Mr. Ahasuerus.

"And?"

"I will be happy to take them off your hands," interjected Kargennian. "But my experience with you in the past has taught me always to ask one question."

"Shoot," said Flint.

"How much?"

"They're on the house," replied Flint.

"I would prefer that you named a price," said Kargennian. "You always do, sooner or later. I would be much happier knowing what you plan to extort from me on the front end."

"You insist?"

"I do."

"Well, partner, what do you think we ought to charge him?"

"I personally would like a cappuccino machine," replied Mr. Ahasuerus. "I have been unable to make anything except rather strong gin with the machine you helped me to build."

"What is a cappuccino machine?" asked Kargennian, puzzled.

"Ask Mr. Romany," said Flint. "He'll know. He can pick it up at the same time he picks up a few cartons of beer and cigarettes."

"That is your asking price?"

"You got it."

"I accept," said Kargennian. "We will sign an agreement to that effect later this evening." He checked his timepiece, a seemingly patternless hodgepodge of dials, tiny lights, numbers, switches, and etched cameos that covered most of his left forearm. "Is it time yet?"

"You mean for Monk and Batman?"

"They are the reason I am here," replied Kargennian.

"I thought it was to tell us how well we're doing," said Flint with a smile. "And to swipe a few more ideas from us."

"You make it very difficult to like you, Mr. Flint," said Kargennian coldly.

"Listen, hotshot," said Flint. "In the two years I've known you you've set up close to fifty Earth games in your goddamned circus, you've palmed off a couple of dozen malcontents and maladroits on our show, you've swiped our animal-training act, and you've tried to buy Billybuck Dancer away four different times. If you liked me much more, I'd go broke."

"Mr. Ahasuerus!" said Kargennian. "Are you going to allow him to insult me like this?"

"He is very versatile," replied the blue man, trying not to display his teeth. "I am sure he could insult you in any manner you wish."

"What?" demanded Kargennian.

"He is my partner," said Mr. Ahasuerus. "Moreover, everything he has said is true. I might wish for more socially acceptable behavior from Mr. Flint—and, to be truthful, I often do—but his veracity is beyond question. The Corporation has really only treated us with civility since we began turning a profit, and when all is said and done, your sole reason for being here is to learn our methods so that you can impress your superiors by turning that same profit elsewhere." He paused, then shrugged. "However, that is neither here nor there. You are our guest, and I for one am delighted to see you again. Would you like the brand name of the cappuccino machine now or later?"

"Later!" snapped Kargennian.

Flint got to his feet. "Come on, hotshot," he said. "Let's get this show on the road. They ought to be in the ring in about ten minutes."

He walked to the door, opened it, and allowed Kargennian to step out ahead of him. Then he turned briefly back to his partner.

"I'll take it from here," he said.

"I was rather hoping that you would," replied the blue man.

"You have qualities, Mr. Ahasuerus."

"I am learning from a master, Mr. Flint," said Mr. Ahasuerus, looking inordinately pleased with himself. "Do try not to insult him past my ability to arrange a reconciliation."

"Partner, you cut me to the quick!" grinned Flint, turning and following the rotund Corporation bureaucrat down the hall to the elevator.

The tent was filled to capacity when they arrived. Flint led Kargennian to the lighting control booth, high above the crowd, where they both sat down and watched Stogie do a ten-minute turn as Harpo Marx.

The audience loved it, though the humor was lost on Kargennian.

Then Tojo switched on the sound system and began speaking, and a moment later Monk, dressed in his buckskins, walked into the cage, took a pair of bows, and directed the robots to let Mickey and Donald out of their crates. He put them through their paces for a few minutes, as Flint explained to Kargennian that these were two of the four animals he would be taking back. Kennedy still hadn't recovered fully, and Nixon worked alone for another two minutes after the catlike creatures were finished.

Then the house lights dimmed, Tojo began speaking again—this time the translated words sounded very much like crushed ice banging against crystal—and suddenly Batman entered the ring.

"This is the one from Sabellius III?" asked Kargennian, as Monk cracked the whip twice and Batman leaped onto a stool.

"Right," said Flint.

A moment later Kargennian actually jumped as Batman hurled himself at Monk and the animal tamer barely escaped the Sabellian's outstretched claws.

"It looks very real," remarked Kargennian, calming down again. "It is very well choreographed."

Monk slashed Batman on the arm, and a trickle of blood began rolling down to his wrist.

"Good art direction, too," remarked Flint dryly.

The performance lasted almost fifteen minutes. Batman dove through hoops, walked a tightrope, juggled, did acrobatics, and made four more attempts to separate Monk's head from his shoulders.

When it was over Monk was bleeding profusely from a gash above his left ear and limping on a leg that had crashed into a metal bar of the cage. He looked like a picture of perfect health compared to Batman.

"Well?" asked Flint, as the crowd began filing out, most of them wandering over to the Dancer's show.

"This has been going on for how many months?" demanded Kargennian.

"Quite a few."

"It's got to stop!"

"It makes money."

"It's the most uncivilized act I have ever seen! No wonder my show has been unable to match your attendance. I would fire anyone who volunteered to be part of such a performance!"

"You're serious, aren't you?" said Flint.

"I was never more serious in my life," answered Kargennian. "These exhibitions of brutality and callousness have got to stop. I am surprised that the Sabellian is still alive!"

"Come by next week," said Flint with a wry grin. "The Sabellian gets to be the trainer."

"I am ordering you to close this show down!"

"Blow it out your ass, hotshot," said Flint. "This show stays open until *we* decide to close it."

"In the name of humanity, I demand—"

"Don't say 'demand,' " said Flint. "It's an ugly word. In fact, coming from you, so's 'humanity.' You're just pissed because you finally figured out that you can't match our gate, and you don't want to look like shit when you go back and tell that to the Corporation. This is *me* you're talking to, not one of those lamebrains back at headquarters."

"I insist that you let me talk to Monk and the Sabellian," said Kargennian. "Once they understand how you have been exploiting them, I am sure they will agree to cease these primitive and vicious displays."

"I'll tell you what," said Flint, amused. "If you can talk them into quitting, I won't stand in your way."

"Let's go!" snapped Kargennian, getting to his feet.

Flint led him back to the mess hall, which was deserted except for the robots that were cleaning the littered tables and scrubbing down the scuff-marked floors, as they did every evening when the staff went to work on the Midway. Then he buzzed Monk's and Batman's rooms on the intercom, and told them to report to him as soon as they had patched up their latest collection of wounds.

Monk showed up first, about twenty minutes later, shirtless, with a towel draped around his shoulders. Batman made his appearance a minute later, still bleeding from a pair of small cuts on his wing membranes. The Sabellian took one look at Monk and promptly moved to the far side of the room.

"Monk, Batman—I'd like you to meet Kargennian," said Flint. "He's an executive with the Corporation, and he just had the privilege of watching you two in action."

Monk mumbled a greeting, while the Sabellian merely folded his arms across his chest and stared at him.

"I'll get right to the point," said Kargennian. "I was completely appalled by what I saw in the ring this evening."

"It's the fucking bat," said Monk. "Six months, and the stupid bastard still can't learn to walk a tightrope."

Batman glared at him, but said nothing.

"You don't understand," continued Kargennian. "Mr. Flint has encouraged this brutality and violence long enough. I want it to cease."

"Bully for you," said Monk with open hostility.

"What goes on in the cage is none of your concern," added Batman.

"I have the power to make you stop," said Kargennian.

"Yeah?" said Monk, taking a couple of steps forward. "That's kind of putting the cart ahead of the horse, ain't it?"

"I don't understand your reference."

"You tell him, Batman," said Monk.

The Sabellian calmly walked over and positioned himself between Kargennian and the doorway. "Having the power to make us stop presupposes that you have the power to leave this room alive," he rumbled ominously.

"But surely you can't *want* to continue performing

in the manner you did tonight!" protested Kargennian.

Flint sat down on a chair, placed his feet on the table and his hands behind his head, and smiled.

"Is this another of *your* ideas, Thaddeus?" demanded Monk.

Flint shook his head. "I'm just an interested bystander."

"Then let me tell you something, shorty," said Monk, returning his attention to Kargennian. "If you don't like what goes on in the cage, all you got to do is come in and throw us out!"

"But—" began Kargennian.

"Unless you would like to pretend this room is the cage," added Batman, advancing a few steps toward the little executive.

"But you can't *want* to—"

"What we want is *our* business," said Monk. "And when we need some fucking bleeding-heart butterball to tell us what we want, we'll send for him. Have you got that straight?"

Kargennian turned to Batman. "Surely," he said, reaching his pudgy arms out supplicatingly, "you cannot agree with this."

"Oh?" said the Sabellian.

"Don't you realize that these people are *using* you, that you are the object of their bigotry?"

"Turn around, Jupiter," said Batman.

Monk took the towel off his shoulders and turned his back to Kargennian. The little executive winced at the multitude of cuts, scars, and welts that crisscrossed the animal tamer's flesh.

"Does he look any more the *user* than the *used*?" demanded Batman coldly.

"You're both crazy!" snapped Kargennian.

"Well, you can't say you weren't warned," said Flint, still smiling. "On the other hand, maybe we ought to keep you around. This is the first time they've agreed on anything in half a year. You just seem to have that effect on people, hotshot."

"You got anything more to say before I lose my temper?" asked Monk.

Kargennian shook his head helplessly, and Monk, giving Batman a wide berth, turned and left the mess hall. The Sabellian followed him a moment later.

"They *enjoy* it!" muttered Kargennian unbelievingly.

"Well, everybody can't be smart like you and me," said Flint with a smile.

"But they'll kill each other as surely as you're sitting there!" persisted Kargennian.

"It's my considered opinion that what they really want to do is *almost* kill each other," replied Flint. "You know, sometimes I'm tempted to drag the two of them to that damned cage when no one is around and just lock them in. I used to have a couple of dogs once—big, ugly mongrels, both males—and for years they kept acting like they wanted to kill each other. You couldn't kennel them together or walk them together or anything—I always had to keep them separated. Then one day I got sick and tired of it, so I put them in a pen together to see what happened."

"And did they fight?"

"You better believe it," said Flint, smiling again at the memory. "They went at it for about five minutes, which is pretty long as dogfights go. But when it was all over they became bosom buddies and never fought again."

"Then why don't you do it with Monk and Batman?" asked Kargennian.

"Because my dogs weren't crazy. Monk and the bat may not *mean* to kill each other, but in case it's escaped your attention, one of them is into pain and the other is an out-and-out looneytoon."

"Surely Monk hasn't always been like this," said the rotund red alien. "Why didn't you nip this attitude at the outset?"

"*What* outset?" demanded Flint irritably. "You don't look at a man and decide that he's sane at three-eighteen on a Tuesday afternoon and mad as a hatter at three-nineteen. People don't make it that easy for you. Maybe Monk was crazy the first time he went into the cage with Batman. Maybe a shrink would say he's still sane; after all, he's only in the cage for a few minutes each day, and the rest of the time he's not all that irrational." Flint sighed. "Look, if everyone who ever went crazy passed out notices and set off rockets to mark the spot, there'd be a lot more people in the funny farms and a lot less working the carnivals." He got to his feet. "Now let's go load those animals."

"Can the show do without them?"

"We've been doing without them for almost a week. The only reason they were in the act tonight was so you'd know I wasn't selling you a bill of goods." He led Kargennian to the door, then turned to the little executive. "I want you to know that there's nothing I'd like better than finding a way to stop the act." He paused. "I also want you to know that if you try to pull any strings to have the Corporation order me to stop it, Monk and Batman will be on the first ship to your home world, and I won't lift a finger to stop them."

Kargennian sighed, and fell into step behind Flint. They spent the next two hours loading the animals onto the ship. Then Kargennian took off, and Flint wandered back to the mess hall, where he found Mr. Ahasuerus waiting for him.

"Is he gone?" asked the blue man.

"Yeah. And before you could tell him what kind of machine you wanted."

"I'll radio him a message," said Mr. Ahasuerus distractedly. "We have a more immediate problem to confront."

"Monk and Batman?" asked Flint wearily.

"Indirectly."

"What's up?"

"I didn't want to mention it while Kargennian was here, but it seems that for the first time in almost three years, we have been run off a planet. Tonight is our last performance on this world."

"Says who?" demanded Flint.

"The local equivalent of the SPCA," said the blue man, his face a cross between irritation and amusement. "It seems that Kargennian wasn't the only person who was distressed by the animal-taming act."

"Can't say that I blame them," said Flint. "Have you offered to close up the specialty show and just run the rest of the carnival?"

"They want us off the planet—lock, stock, and barrel, to borrow one of your expressions."

"Did it ever occur to you," said Flint, "that these guys are getting to be more trouble than they're worth, money or no money?"

"Possibly the next world will be different," said Mr. Ahasuerus.

He had no idea how prophetic his words were.

17.

Mr. Ahasuerus was supervising the construction of the Midway when Flint approached him. He gave a final order to one of the robots, put his pad of notepaper away, and turned to face his partner.

"Yes, Mr. Flint. What can I do for you?"

"You can tell me that you can get along without me for a few hours," replied Flint.

"Certainly," said the blue man. "Is something wrong?"

"No. I just thought I'd borrow one of the landrovers and drive into town with Diggs and Tojo."

The blue man looked his surprise. "You have studiously avoided visiting local municipalities ever since we played our first two worlds," he pointed out.

"That's because you have studiously avoided landing on any planets that were worth the effort. This makes the forty-third world we've played, and it's the first goddamned one that looks like an alien planet is supposed to look."

"Oh?" said Mr. Ahasuerus dryly. "And how does an alien planet look?"

"Well, for starters, *different.* This one looks like the covers of all the magazines I used to read when I was a kid; the others all looked like the cover of *Farmer's Life.*"

"And you feel that that makes this world more interesting?"

"Even *you* have got to be getting tired of wheat fields and drainage ditches," said Flint. He gestured to the city, which was clearly discernible some twenty miles away. "Look at that thing! Huge buildings, and weird-looking aircars buzzing all the hell over, and ramps hundreds of feet above the ground. Aren't you even curious to see what a real city looks like?"

"I've *seen* a real city," said the blue man. "I am more concerned with the people who inhabit it."

"After a while, one mark gets to looking pretty much like another, no matter what world they come from," said Flint. "Maybe I'll feel the same about cities one of these days, but you've got to admit you haven't given me an awful lot of opportunity to get tired of them."

"Well, you're certainly welcome to go into it and see for yourself," said Mr. Ahasuerus. "I should point out to you, though, that I know almost nothing about Kamanetrii V. I booked us in here because it was the only world that would take us on such short notice, after we were forced to vacate our last location so prematurely. I do not, in truth, even know what the inhabitants look like, though of course I shall find out from my computer when I return to my office."

"How about the translators?" asked Flint. "Are they rigged for Kamanetrii yet?"

"Certainly. That was the very first thing I ordered done when I knew we would be landing here."

"Good. Then I'll see you later this afternoon."

Flint turned to leave.

"Do be careful, Mr. Flint. This is, when all is said and done, a totally unfamiliar world."

"You've been reading too many potboilers, Mr. Ahasuerus," said Flint with a smile. "Nobody's going to harm us."

"That was not exactly what I had in mind," admitted the blue man.

"Relax. The Carnies' First Commandment is that you never offend a mark until he's spent all his money."

Flint returned to the ship, picked up a trio of translating devices, stopped by the mess hall to inform Diggs and Tojo that he was ready to go, and was soon driving one of the battery-powered landrovers toward the city.

"It's even bigger than I thought," remarked Diggs as they pulled to within a mile of it. "The damned thing must house ten million people."

"Or half a dozen very large ones," said Flint, making a conscious attempt not to be overawed by the towering structures.

"What the hell are all those things?" asked Diggs, pointing at a spot about two hundred yards above the ground.

"They look like ramps," answered Flint. "But that doesn't make any sense. See how far they jut out past the buildings? Why would anyone go that far past a door?"

"Are they streets?" asked Tojo, squinting his narrow eyes and peering at the structures in question.

"I don't think so," said Diggs. "I can't see any traffic moving on them. Most of the cars seem to be flying, or hanging upside down on monorails." He shook his head. "Besides, they don't have any retaining walls. Too easy for a car to skid off—or a person, for that matter."

"Well, maybe they're just for looks, then," said Flint.

"Uh-uh," said Diggs. "They look too functional to be just for decoration. Besides, they're not all that pretty."

"Maybe a Kamanetriian thinks they look like Jayne Mansfield," said Flint. "Who the hell knows? And while we're on the subject of things we don't know, I don't imagine anyone here can read their traffic signs."

"I haven't seen one," said Diggs, "but I think that's a pretty safe assumption."

"Then maybe we'd better park the landrover outside the city so we don't break any laws," said Flint. He paused for a moment. "Shit! We should have brought Max along."

"Stogie? What the hell for?"

"Because he goes into every town we hit and leads them back to the show. Maybe he could give us some pointers."

"He never saw a city like this one, Thaddeus," said Diggs. "Most of 'em look like Skokie or Palo Alto."

"Has anyone else noticed that there don't seem to be any suburbs?" remarked Tojo. "Just scrubland and cultivated fields, and then suddenly you're in the city."

"Yeah. That *is* kind of strange, isn't it?" said Flint. He pulled up next to what seemed to be a door through one of the huge buildings, skidded to a halt, and got out of the vehicle.

"Should we lock it?" asked Tojo.

Flint looked down fondly at the hunchback. "You amaze me sometimes, Tojo, you really do. Here we are, the first human beings ever to walk into this city, and you're worrying about leaving the goddamned car unlocked."

He shook his head in amusement, then turned and, followed by Diggs and Tojo, passed through a portal that seemed to lead inside the city.

The portal turned out to be a long corridor, flanked by numerous metal doors and an occasional shop window which displayed a vast array of items that made absolutely no sense to them.

"Stores?" asked Diggs.

"Looks like," agreed Flint. "Though who the hell would want to buy any of this shit is beyond me." He paused in front of a window. "If I didn't know better, I'd swear this joint was selling ten thousand varieties of rubber balls. Can you see anything else in there?"

Diggs and Tojo looked in and were forced to agree with Flint.

"Maybe they all play soccer," suggested Diggs with a shrug.

"One of those balls had to be five feet across," replied Flint. "I'd hate to meet the guy who can kick *that* around."

He turned away from the window and began walking again, just in time to collide with an alien that seemed to resemble nothing more than a flesh-and-blood Humpty Dumpty. It stood perhaps five feet tall, was completely round, possessed two arms and two legs, each with opposing thumbs, and was covered with soft white down. Its eyes were large and blue, its nose almost nonexistent, its mouth broad and rosy-lipped. And, Flint noted without surprise, it was totally naked.

"Sorry," said Flint, reaching out to help the being to its feet. "Are you okay?"

The alien let out a shriek and jumped back to avoid Flint's hands.

"What the hell's the matter?" muttered Flint, frowning.

"Turn on your translator," said Tojo. "He doesn't understand you."

Flint flicked on the mechanism. "Please don't be afriad," he said. "We are visitors from the carnival."

The alien calmed down almost instantly.

"I apologize for my clumsiness," it said. "You startled me when you spoke in your native tongue." It paused. "You bear a striking resemblance to certain . . . well, let us not go into it." It paused again. "So you are from the carnival outside the city? How pleased I am to meet you. I was planning on taking my"—the word he uttered was untranslatable—"to see you tonight."

"Good," said Flint, pulling one of his ever-present free passes out of his pocket and handing it to the alien. "Use this ticket when you go."

"Thank you," said the alien, immediately slipping the ticket into its mouth.

"Did he eat it?" whispered Diggs.

"How the hell do I know?" responded Flint. He turned back to the alien. "We are strangers to your city, but we thought we'd like to do a little sightseeing before returning to the show. Can you direct us to the kind of places that tourists usually go?"

The alien launched into a long and complicated

description of his city, about every third term of which was untranslatable. Finally Flint interrupted to thank him, and started walking off in the direction he had originally been going.

"What the hell *are* they?" asked Diggs. "Humanoid or what?"

"Who knows?" shrugged Flint. "I expect to see one of them falling off a wall any minute now."

"Monk and Batman are gonna want to know," persisted Diggs. "Which one gets to be the trainer?"

"These are the least human-looking batch of aliens I've seen yet," said Flint. "I guess that makes the bat the trainer."

"They don't look any more like Batman than like Monk," said Tojo.

"We'll worry about it later," said Flint, emerging from the corridor into a large open area. It began as a square, quickly opened out into a trapezoid, and wound up as a huge semicircle some quarter-mile in diameter. There were no streets or sidewalks, but the scores of egglike aliens who were walking through it seemed to follow preset paths, and such minimal vehicular traffic as they could see seemed to observe no paths or patterns whatsoever.

"This is getting a little too strange for my taste," muttered Diggs, looking at the architecture and trying fruitlessly to make some kind of sense out of it. Everything had been created at angles—doors, windows, decorations—and no two angles seemed to fit together. Traffic raced around on monorails or in the air, rising and falling several hundred feet precipitously in no discernible pattern. A vast array of signs, some neon, some in almost blindingly bright blinking lights, hung over shop windows, music blared and mingled with the traffic noises, vendors marched in and out of formation hawking their totally incomprehensible wares. Here and there they could see members of races that were obviously not native to the planet going about their business, but they couldn't begin to understand what their business was.

"Now I know what *sensory overload* means," said Diggs grimly. "Let's go home, Thaddeus."

"Take it easy," said Flint. "They're just marks."

"I ain't ever seen a mark that looked like a hard-boiled egg before!" said Diggs devoutly. "This place is *weird*!"

"Look," said Flint patiently. "They've got stores, don't they? That means they spend money. Everything else is window dressing. This is just a bunch of aborigine huts writ big."

"It's fascinating!" said Tojo, gaping at his surroundings.

"Close your mouth," said Flint with a smile. "One of these guys might shove a ticket into it."

"What if one of them hassles us?" persisted Diggs.

"Why would they?" said Flint, starting forward.

"But *if* one of them does!"

"Crack him open and fry him," said Flint.

He set out across the open area, followed by Tojo, whose small eyes were wide in rapt fascination. Diggs watched them for a moment, then sighed and broke into a run until he had caught up with them.

"I wish I had brought my camera!" said Tojo.

"If you can find something that looks like a drugstore or a gift shop, maybe you can pick up a postcard," said Flint.

"It wouldn't be the same," replied Tojo. "Besides, I didn't bring any money."

"Neither did I, now that you come to mention it," remarked Flint. "I hope there's no parking meter out by the landrover."

After a quarter of an hour they began to get the feel of the place, to see certain patterns where none had been evident before. Flint kept introducing himself to the egg-shaped aliens and passing out free tickets, all of which were immediately inserted into happy, smiling mouths.

"Remind me to check the gate tonight," he remarked to Tojo. "I've *got* to find out if they have carrying pouches in there, or if they're actually eating the damned things."

They walked for a few more minutes, and finally Flint came to a halt.

"I've seen enough," he announced. "Nine restaurants, a couple of game arcades, an ad for what looks like a Sumo wrestling match. We'll do okay on this world." He looked around at his surroundings. "It's not so complicated once you get used to it. Hell, I could probably hack a cab around here in a week's time."

Diggs was certain that they were hopelessly lost and would have to solicit help to find their way back, and even Tojo seemed unsure of his bearings, but Flint led them directly to the landrover in ten minutes.

"How did you find it so easily?" Tojo inquired.

"Piece of cake," said Flint, displaying the pocket knife he had hidden in his hand. "I put scratch marks on the lampposts, or whatever the hell they were."

"The landrover has a homing signal," said Tojo.

"I don't trust Mr. Ahasuerus' machines," said Flint. "His computer is supposed to know how to spell, too."

"I just hope they don't send a lynching party out after us for defacing public property," said Diggs. He shuddered inadvertently. "God, I'm glad to be out of that place!"

"What the hell's the matter with you, Rigger?" demanded Flint as he climbed into the landrover and started the engine. "I thought you were supposed to be the unflappable type."

"I don't know."

"That's no answer," said Flint. "It's not as if you haven't seen some pretty odd-looking aliens before. I've seen you sit down and play poker with half a dozen guys that make King Kong look like a faggot."

"Yeah," said Diggs. "But I always saw 'em on *my* turf, playing *my* games. When I walked into that city,

I suddenly realized just how far from home we really were."

"It's a little late in the game to be having second thoughts," said Flint with a smile.

"Home doesn't mean Earth," said Diggs. "Home means the carny."

"Then you were only half an hour away."

"Half an hour, half the universe—it comes to the same thing," said Diggs. "I don't know if I can explain it, Thaddeus, but I'll try. You spend enough time with the carny and you forget what real people are like. Oh, you see them when they come to the Midway, but you see them as marks. You get to forgetting that there's a world out there that doesn't even know you're alive, that doesn't care if you can roll thirty sevens in a row or deal four royal flushes from a freshly opened deck. *We're* the freaks, not them, and I don't like to be reminded of it."

"Are you trying to tell me that you'd have been just as scared in Boston or Boise?" asked Flint.

"I think so. We belong out by county fairgrounds, Thaddeus. The marks should come to us. It's not good for us to see where they live." He paused for a moment. "I'm fifty-six years old, and I've been a gambler and a carny since I was seventeen. I don't like to see all the things I never did." He looked over toward Flint. "Didn't it bother you, seeing all that?"

"No, Rigger, it didn't." Flint ran a hand through his thick hair. "Maybe it will when I'm fifty-six. Right now all I see is a city that isn't half as different as I expected." He shrugged. "Maybe the skeleton isn't as dumb as I thought. What would a totally alien city want with a carnival, anyway?"

"I thought it was—" began Tojo.

"Yeah, I know," interrupted Flint. "You thought it was fascinating. Remember to bring your camera when we come back tomorrow."

"You're coming back?" demanded Diggs.

"I never found out what those ramps were. You got me interested."

"You could have asked someone," said Diggs. "What's the *real* reason?"

"This was the first time in half a year that I've been able to spend four whole hours without thinking about Monk and the bat," said Flint. "I liked it." He paused to light a cigarette. "Not everyone wants to hide in the carnival, Rigger. Some of us like to get away from all the freaks every now and then. Those Humpty Dumpties were kind of interesting."

"They were strange," said Diggs.

"Always assuming that they're sane, you've got a lot more in common with them than with a couple of performers I could name."

Flint became more and more irritable as the landrover approached the ship, so much so that neither Tojo nor Diggs spoke during the last ten minutes.

Mr. Ahasuerus was coming out of the ship as Flint, after parking the vehicle, was going in.

"Ah, Mr. Flint!" the blue man greeted him. "I trust you enjoyed your sojourn?"

"It was okay," said Flint.

"And what did you think of your exotic, alien city?"

Flint looked from his partner to the enormous megalopolis shimmering in the distance, and then back.

"It wasn't worth the wait," he said. "It's filled with people, just like any other city."

"I could have told you," said Mr. Ahasuerus.

"I suppose you could have," said Flint. Then he shrugged. "Let's get to work."

18.

"Well?" asked Flint, looking across the room at his partner, and trying not to wince at the blue man's latest painting, which held a place of honor directly to the left of his desk.

"I really can't say, Mr. Flint," replied Mr. Ahasuerus, drumming his fingers lightly on his desktop. "Even my computer can offer us no help."

"Somehow I'm not surprised," commented Flint dryly.

"Evidently the Gorbites resemble Men and Sabellians equally."

"Which is to say, not at all," replied Flint. "I told you that when I got back. They look like they ought to be packed twelve to a carton and put in a refrigerator."

"I am totally unable to come to a decision," said the blue man.

"Why should today be different from any other?" muttered Flint. He lit a cigarette. "Listen, one of 'em has got to be the trainer and one of 'em has got to be the animal. Why don't we just flip a coin and tell them it was the computer's decision?"

"That would be unethical," said Mr. Ahasuerus gravely.

"You think it's more ethical to let Monk and the bat go a quick fifteen or twenty rounds trying to decide who cracks the whip?" replied Flint. "Hell, they could kill each other before they even get in the cage."

"I am open to alternatives."

"I should sure as hell hope so!" said Flint irritably.

"Have you any?" asked Mr. Ahasuerus.

"I'm working on it," said Flint. "In the meantime, maybe you can tell me why the hell we're calling these things Gorbites instead of Kamanetriians."

"Because that's what they call themselves," replied the blue man. "Why are you called a Man instead of a Terran or an Earthling?"

"I'm not fussy. Call me anything you want."

"You're being difficult again, Mr. Flint," sighed Mr. Ahasuerus.

"I'm sorry," said Flint with a mild attempt at sincerity. "It's just that we seem to have a little problem here that's going to become a big one before it goes away."

"Possibly we should consult Jupiter and Batman," suggested the blue man.

"Do you honestly believe that either of them will volunteer to be the animal?" said Flint. Suddenly he blinked, as if the idea appealed to him. "You know, they're both so much into this macho shit that one of them just might volunteer at that!"

"Shall I summon them?" asked Mr. Ahasuerus.

"It can't hurt," replied Flint.

Batman arrived first, surveyed the office briefly, and walked over to one of the blue man's more abstract pieces of furniture. He sat down, carefully spreading his wing membranes to avoid impaling them on a couple of jutting decorations, and turned to Flint.

"You had something to discuss with me?"

"In a minute," replied Flint. "We're waiting for someone."

"Who?"

"Your very favorite person."

"Why do you delight in being rude to me, Mr. Flint?" asked Batman.

"I haven't given it much thought. Probably it's because I don't like you very much."

"I have never asked for your friendship."

"Well, cheer up then," said Flint. "You don't have it."

"I cannot help wondering if Kargennian was correct, and that this represents racial bigotry on your part," continued the Sabellian.

"It's only racial bigotry if all the other bats are like you," said Flint.

"I do not understand."

"That's not my problem," said Flint. He snuffed his cigarette out and lit another just as Monk entered the office.

"Good evening, Jupiter," said Mr. Ahasuerus.

"What's this all about?" demanded Monk.

"Didn't you bring the cards and the poker chips?" asked Flint innocently.

Monk glared at him for a moment and then sat on the chair that was farthest from Batman.

"What's up?" said Monk. "We've got to start getting ready for the show."

"That's what we are here to discuss," said the blue man.

"What's to talk about?" asked Monk. "We're on in less than two hours."

"True," agreed Batman. "I must begin getting into my costume."

"What costume are you talking about?" demanded Monk. "*I'm* doing the training tonight."

"I do believe you boys have come right to the heart of the matter," grinned Flint. "Jupiter, what makes you think you're doing the training?"

"I talked to Tojo when you got back this afternoon. He told me that the Kamanetriians don't look anything like Batman."

"True," admitted Flint.

"Diggs told me that they bear no resemblance to Men," interjected Batman hotly.

"Also true," said Flint. "Do you begin to see that we might have an interesting situation on our hands?"

"The computer says that you are both equally removed from the Gorbites," added Mr. Ahasuerus.

"Who the hell are the Gorbites?" demanded Monk.

"That's what the natives call themselves," replied the blue man.

"Dumb name," muttered Monk.

"There is really no problem," said Batman. "Monk was the trainer on the last world, so by rights it should now be my turn."

"No way!" snapped Monk. "The agreement was that you'd be the trainer on worlds where they looked more like you than like me—and on this world they don't."

"They also don't look more like you," said Batman coldly. "It is my turn."

"Fuck you!" yelled Monk. "Turns ain't got nothing to do with it!"

"Possibly you can think of some better way of determining it," said Batman, rising ominously to his feet.

"You bet your ass I can!" said Monk, also standing up.

"Mr. Flint," said the blue man hastily, "I told you this might happen."

"Knock it off!" snapped Flint in a voice that somehow received their instant attention. "You've got two choices. You can come up with a peaceful solution to the problem, or you can both stay in the ship until we hit the next world. There's no third way."

"Are you threatening us?" asked Batman emotionlessly.

"The time for threats is past," said Flint. "I'm telling it like it is. You confine your heroics to the cage or you sit this out." He looked at each of them in turn. "Without pay."

"You're bluffing," said Monk without conviction.

"Not this time, Jupiter," replied Flint. "Mr. Ahasuerus and I can't make the decision on who trains and who doesn't. Now, do you need that damned cage bad enough to make it for us?"

"You can't take it away from me!" growled Monk, suddenly looking like a hunted animal. "It's mine!"

Flint turned to the Sabellian. "Do you agree?"

"If Monk is willing to perform, I will not be the first to back down," said Batman. "We will reach a decision."

Flint looked at his watch. "You've got twenty minutes."

Monk and Batman filed out, never touching one another, and the door slid shut behind them.

"He's like a goddamned drug addict!" said Flint disgustedly. "Look at his eyes when you threaten to take his cage away—suddenly he's got wall-to-wall pupils."

"I wonder if this is the best way to handle the situation, Mr. Flint," said the blue man.

"Probably not," admitted Flint. "But it's the best way *I* know how, and that's what it always seems to come down to. Got a cup of coffee?"

"Columbian or Jamaican?" asked the blue man, walking to his cabinet.

"Black," was the response.

Flint had just finished his coffee and was starting on a second cup when Monk reentered the office.

"Well?"

"We've come up with a plan, if you'll go for it," said Monk.

"Let's hear it."

"What if we traded roles every night?"

Flint lowered his head in thought for a moment. "Not bad," he said at last. "I was toying with something like that a couple of months back—letting the audience know what was going on—but the skeleton here talked me out of it. Does Batman agree?"

"Yes."

"We're booked here for nine days. Who works the extra performance?"

"We'll worry about that when we come to it," answered Monk.

"I see you're about as farsighted as usual," said Flint. Then he shrugged. "Well, what the hell—why not? You'll both stay a bit healthier that way. And who knows? Maybe we can stir up a little extra publicity with this gimmick. After all, we didn't have much chance to do our advance work on this dirtball."

"Then it's a deal?" asked Monk.

"Yeah. Who's the trainer tonight?"

"Batman. It's his turn."

"I thought turns didn't count," said Flint.

"That's when *my* turn was two weeks off," answered Monk.

He turned and left the office, and Flint finished drinking his coffee.

"Do you think it will work?" asked the blue man.

"As long as those two idiots keep ripping each other to shreds in the cage, *anything* we try will work," said Flint decisively. "And maybe this way they won't take such a sustained beating."

For the first four nights nothing out of the ordinary took place: the two specialty tents played to capacity audiences, the games made money, the rides edged above their break-even point, and Julius Squeezer was back to baiting the weaklings in the crowd.

On the fifth night, Flint noticed that a number of the Gorbites took pennants and banners into the animal-training tent, and by the sixth, seventh, and eighth the grandstand resembled a football stadium on Super Bowl day, with howling partisans cheering for their favorite and heaping abuse upon the enemy. Monk and Batman reveled in it, and Flint decided that he would soon have to order an even bigger tent from Kargennian.

And so they came to the ninth day.

19.

The little hunchback, dressed in one of his gaudier outfits, scuttled across the sawdust floor of the specialty tent, made his way through the incoming throngs of Gorbites, and climbed the unsteady ladder to the lighting booth, where Flint and Mr. Ahasuerus were sitting and waiting for the final performance on Kamanetrii V to begin.

"Thaddeus," he stammered breathlessly, "I think we may have a problem."

"What's up?" asked Flint.

"I think you'd better come backstage with me," said Tojo. "You, too, Mr. Ahasuerus."

"I don't play guessing games," said Flint. "What's going on?"

"It's Monk and Batman."

"Of course it's Monk and Batman," replied Flint irritably. "What's the matter this time?"

"They're both dressed," said Tojo.

"I was wondering how long it would take them to get around to this."

"I am afraid I do not understand," said the blue man.

"You will," said Flint, getting to his feet and following Tojo down the ladder.

Mr. Ahasuerus fell into step behind them, and a moment later the three of them were confronting Monk and Batman in the waiting area just outside the ring.

Monk was resplendent in his buckskins, and had borrowed a banner from one of his boosters in the crowd, which he wore wrapped around his waist. The Sabellian was wearing his silver lamé cutoff overalls, and had added a pair of bright-green patent-leather boots to the outfit.

"What the hell is *that* supposed to say?" asked Flint, gesturing to the banner.

"I didn't have my translator with me," said Monk. "But I imagine it either means *Long Live Me* or *Death to Batman.* Either way, I'll settle."

"So much for pleasantries," said Flint. "What's the script for tonight?"

"Well," answered Monk, "we figured that as long as everyone in the crowd knows we're both intelligent, and since we've split the duties dead even so far, and since this is the last night . . . well, we thought we'd put a new wrinkle in the act."

"There's a difference between being sentient and being intelligent," said Flint dryly. "But let it pass."

"Anyway, we thought as long as we've both got fans out there and we're not fooling anyone about what we are, we'd take turns being the trainer."

"Do you mean that you plan to change roles with every trick?" asked Mr. Ahasuerus.

"That's exactly what he means," said Flint.

"Then *that's* why you're both in costume!" exclaimed the blue man.

"You're a little slow on the uptake tonight," commented Flint. He turned to Monk and Batman. "Tools?"

"Just a whip," said Monk.

"You didn't bring your joystick?" persisted Flint, staring at the Sabellian.

"I will not need it," replied Batman coldly.

"Should we permit it, Mr. Flint?" asked the blue man.

"I'm thinking about it," replied Flint, rubbing his chin thoughtfully while looking from one performer to the other.

"Well, you can stop your thinking right now!" snapped Monk. "We do it our way or we don't go on, and you get to tell six thousand animated eggs that they ain't gonna see a show."

Flint looked calmly at Monk for a long minute. Finally he nodded. "You've got forty-five minutes," he said.

He turned and began walking back to the lighting booth, Mr. Ahasuerus at his heels, while Tojo went over to his announcer's stand and started checking the sound system.

"That was very unlike you, Mr. Flint," remarked the blue man.

"Yeah?"

"Yes. I have seen people try to pressure you before."

"And you think I let them blackmail me into letting them go on?" asked Flint.

"It is so unlike you that I do not know what to think," admitted Mr. Ahasuerus.

Flint stopped walking and turned to face his partner. "This thing has finally come to a head. Let's let them have it out and get it over with."

"You were expecting this all along?"

"Weren't you?" asked Flint. He looked around the stands. "Jesus! It looks like a Roman coliseum!" He continued walking to the booth.

The blue man joined him a minute later, and they took their seats. Then the lights dimmed, Tojo began speaking into the microphone, and a moment later Stogie was dropping silverware all over the sawdust and trying to ride a bicycle that kept falling apart quicker than he could put it together.

The audience applauded politely, but there was no doubt that they were waiting for their two gladiators to emerge. Stogie sensed their restlessness, and cut his act short.

"Give me your translator," said Flint.

"But you *never* use a translator!" said Mr. Ahasuerus.

"I never gave a damn what Tojo said before," replied Flint, taking the mechanism from the blue man. He flicked on the power and leaned back as the little hunchback turned on his microphone again.

"And now, ladies and gentlemen," cried Tojo, "the moment you have all been waiting for, the moment we have been building up to for nine days—the Battle of the Ages!"

There was a wild scream from the crowd as Monk and Batman emerged through the tent flap and walked to the door of the cage.

"Presenting, from Earth, Jupiter Monk, the most famous and fearless animal tamer in the galaxy!"

Monk took a step forward and bowed slightly, as the audience hooted with pleasure.

"And from Sabellius III, the bravest of the brave, the meanest of the mean, the cruelest of the cruel—I give you Batman!"

A cry of equal volume erupted as Batman stepped forward and bowed with a flourish, drawing his wing membranes about him as if they were a cape.

"Prepare yourselves for a spectacle of unprecedented passion and power!" cried Tojo, the translating mechanism masking his stammer and somehow reproducing his alliteration. "Each of these two magnificent showmen will, by turn, attempt to master the most dangerous beast they have ever been forced to face. Each will put his safety, and even his life, on the line. Each will perform feats of death-defying dexterity. And now"—he paused momentarily while a prerecorded drumroll filled the tent—"let the battle begin!"

"Not bad," commented Flint, handing the translator back to Mr. Ahasuerus.

"I only hope he was overstating the case," said the blue man devoutly.

"Well," said Flint, focusing his attention on the cage, "you can hope."

20.

Monk walked into the cage, slammed the door in Batman's face, and walked to the far side of it. The Sabellian entered a moment later, and signaled Tojo to latch the door.

"There will be no leaving until this matter is finally settled," said Batman coldly.

"The only way *you're* leaving is on a stretcher," replied Monk. He turned his back to the Sabellian and carefully wrapped his whip around one of the bars. "Let's get this show on the road."

The Sabellian unfurled his own whip. "You wish to be the animal first?"

"Whether you're doing tricks or holding a whip, there's only one animal in here," grated Monk. "And I'm looking at him."

"We shall see," said Batman, flicking out his whip and driving Monk onto a stool. He walked to the trunk and pulled out three hard rubber balls, tossing them to Monk in rapid succession. Monk dropped the third, and the whip snaked out and bit through his shirt, opening a gash on his shoulder.

Monk began juggling, and had just worked into a proper rhythm when Batman tossed yet another ball to him. Monk tried to catch it, lost his concentration, and suddenly all four balls fell to the floor. He began picking them up as the whip reached out and landed on his back.

Then, before Batman could react, Monk hurled one of the balls at the Sabellian as hard as he could. It caught him on the shin. The whip fell from

Batman's hand as he clutched at his leg, and he quickly looked across the ring, anticipating an attack.

"Not yet, you son of a bitch," Monk said with a harsh grin. He climbed back onto the stool. "Let's give 'em their money's worth before we put you out of your misery."

Batman picked up the balls, returned them to Monk, and allowed him to finish the trick without further harassment. Then he walked to the door, hung up his whip, and waited, arms folded, while Monk retrieved his own whip.

Monk drove the Sabellian to the highest stool in the cage, picked up a small hoop, set it ablaze, and stood some ten feet away.

"That is too far," said Batman.

The whip slashed out, ripping into the Sabellian's wing membrane.

"I don't believe I heard you," said Monk.

Batman said nothing further, but instead leaned forward, stretched his arms ahead of him, and leaped. Monk realized that the Sabellian was diving at him rather than the hoop, and he quickly stepped backward, laughing aloud as Batman hit the canvas with a resounding thud.

"Fucking amateur!"

He turned away to hang up his whip, and the Sabellian reached out and grabbed his leg, sending him to the floor as well. He was on his feet in an instant, but by then Batman was also standing.

"My turn," whispered the Sabellian.

Monk slowly unclenched his fists and tossed his whip up against the bars. Batman began walking across the ring to retrieve his own whip and Monk helped him along with a foot in the small of his back.

The crowd screamed—it had been cheering right along, but this particular noise was ugly enough to catch Monk's attention—and he turned to them and made an obscene gesture.

A moment later Batman had him balancing precariously on a tightrope. Just as he was approaching the end of the stunt, the Sabellian reached out and hit the rope with his whip handle, and Monk, after waving his arms wildly while trying to maintain his balance, fell to the floor.

The crowd voiced another cry of outrage, and this time it was the Sabellian who addressed it with a gesture that only Monk, who had spent long weeks in a spaceship with him, understood.

Monk drove Batman around the ring a couple of times, slashing him twice before finally choosing a stool for him, and Tojo put his face up against the bars of the cage.

"Take it easy, Jupiter!" he stammered. "You two will kill each other!"

Monk raked his whip over the bars, barely missing Tojo's face.

"You keep out of this, dwarf!" he snapped.

Then he turned back to Batman, grinned evilly, and pointed toward the trapeze that was suspended from the top of the cage. The Sabellian pulled himself up onto it and suddenly, before Monk could give his next command, he launched himself at the animal tamer in earnest. The two fell to the canvas and rolled over and over, biting, scratching, gouging. They separated as they hit the door and Monk, regaining his feet first, delivered a heavy kick to the Sabellian's ribs as the noise level in the tent continued to grow.

"The trapeze, you fucking bat!" he growled, wiping the blood from his mouth and nose.

Batman worked the trapeze, and Monk ran the football course through flaming hoops, and Batman walked the tightrope, and Monk went through a tumbling run.

Both were bleeding from numerous cuts and gashes, and each had attacked the other twice. The crowd was going wild, each member screaming the name of his favorite, roaring enthusiastically as each blow fell.

Tojo, standing a few feet away from the cage, checked his watch and found, to his surprise, that they still had twenty-eight minutes to go. Suddenly the hunchback was aware of an added presence, and turned to see the blue man standing beside him.

"We've got to make them stop!" said Mr. Ahasuerus. "They're killing each other!"

"I know," said Tojo. "I've been trying to get their attention, but they won't look at me."

The blue man stepped up to the bars. "Jupiter!" he called.

Monk, his face a bloody mask, turned and glared at him.

"Jupiter, this has got to stop!"

Monk screamed something unintelligible and turned back to Batman, who was attempting to juggle four balls.

"I'm ordering you to stop!" commanded the blue man, struggling to be heard over the frenzied screaming of the crowd.

Monk turned to him again, and as he did so the Sabellian hurled a ball at him, catching him in the small of the back. He bellowed a curse, picked the ball up, and threw it at the blue man's head. It bounced off the bars and rolled across the ring. Monk suddenly seemed totally unaware of it, and turned his efforts to trying to make Batman drop one of the remaining three balls.

Then it was Batman's turn to wield the whip, and Mr. Ahasuerus worked his way around the cage to where the Sabellian stood.

"Please!" he entreated. "This has ceased to be entertainment!"

"It never was," panted the Sabellian, flicking the whip in Monk's direction.

"I implore you . . ."

"If you try to stop us," said the Sabellian, "I will kill you."

Mr. Ahasuerus stepped back, then walked around to where Tojo stood.

"They're both out of control," he said desperately. "What can we do?"

"Where's Thaddeus?" asked the hunchback, wincing as the Sabellian raked the whip handle across Monk's face.

"In the booth. He refuses to intervene."

"Maybe you'd better talk to him again," said Tojo. "I don't think either of them can last another ten minutes."

"I think that's what he's hoping."

"I don't mean that they won't be able to perform," said Tojo. "I mean I think they'll be dead."

Mr. Ahasuerus took one last look at the cage, where Monk had lifted a stool high above his head and hurled it at the Sabellian, and raced back to the lighting-control booth.

"Mr. Flint!" he cried. "We've got to do something!"

"We are," said Flint. "We're letting them have what they've been asking for."

"But they'll kill each other!"

"Then they'll kill each other," replied Flint harshly. "Whatever the hell happens, I want this goddamned thing resolved tonight!"

"But—"

"Shut up and watch the show."

Mr. Ahasuerus seemed about to say something further. Then he sighed and sat down next to his partner, watching miserably as Monk and Batman took turns cutting each other to shreds to the deafening shrieks of their partisans.

After another five minutes both participants seemed to slow down perceptibly, and a moment later all attempts at performing tricks were abandoned. Monk hurled himself at the Sabellian again, and this time, as they got to their feet, neither made any pretense of continuing the act. Monk landed a solid right to Batman's jaw. The Sabellian took it without blinking and responded by driving his knee into his smaller antagonist's belly.

They broke apart then, and a moment later were hurling stools, and any other prop they could lift, at each other. The screams of the crowd were deafening.

Monk spit out a tooth, picked up his whip by the cutting end, and swung it around his head, catching Batman in the temple with the handle. The Sabellian responded by grabbing it before Monk could drag it out of reach, and with a quick jerk he pulled the whip out of Monk's hands.

Now Batman was in possession of both whips, and he began driving Monk to the far side of the ring. Monk picked up a stool and tried to use it to fend off the snaking, biting leather, but the Sabellian pierced his guard more and more frequently until one of the whips curled around the leg of the stool and ripped it away, leaving Monk defenseless.

Flint got to his feet.

"I think it's time," he said, starting to climb down the ladder. "Call the cops, and have Tojo get Julius and the Dancer in here quick."

When he got to the floor of the tent, the crowd was turning ugly. He couldn't understand what they were shouting, but there was no doubt about their mood. Competition, no matter how brutal, was exciting; slaughter evidently was not.

Suddenly one of the Gorbites raced out of the grandstand and ran to the cage before anyone could stop him. He opened the door and threw himself at Batman's back, knocking the surprised Sabellian to the floor.

"What the fuck is going on?" yelled Monk through battered lips.

The Gorbite jabbered something to him that he couldn't understand.

"Who invited *you* in?" roared Monk, outraged. "This is a *private* war!"

The Gorbite said something else, then turned and drove his foot into Batman's side.

Monk picked up a stool and slammed it into his face. The Gorbite fell senseless to the canvas.

"When I want your fucking help, I'll ask for it!" he snarled.

A hush had fallen over the crowd when the Gorbite

had entered the ring. Now a mean, ugly murmur began spreading through it, rising to a hideous crescendo, and before Flint was fully aware of what was happening, another twenty of the Gorbites were charging toward the cage.

And suddenly Billybuck Dancer was standing by the door, his hands on his hips, watching the charging aliens with a detached curiosity.

"Fire into the air, Dancer!" shouted Flint. "Don't kill any of them!"

The Dancer drew his pistol and fired it twice. A couple of the Gorbites stopped momentarily, but most of them never hesitated in their frenzy to get to the cage.

Flint became aware of a huge green presence beside him.

"Should I try to stop them?" asked Julius Squeezer.

"It's too late," said Flint. "Besides, if we're going to have a riot, let's try to confine it to the cage."

Two Gorbites had already passed through the door, and then seven more joined them before the Dancer slammed it shut and fired another half-dozen shots at the stampeding crowd's feet.

"Keep out of this, you bastards!" screamed Monk, leaping into the middle of the Gorbites and striking them right and left. An instant later one of them grabbed his feet and he momentarily vanished from sight. Then Batman began bringing his whip down on the egglike beings, and suddenly they parted. The Sabellian raced over to Monk and pulled him to his feet.

"Keep out of this!" hissed Batman to the Gorbites. "This is none of your affair."

They charged the two performers, and Monk and Batman, standing shoulder to shoulder, fought back as best they could. For a moment Flint thought they would come out of it intact, but then one of the Gorbites got his hands on a whip, and two more began hurling stools and props.

"You stupid bastards!" bellowed Monk. "Who asked you to—"

A whip wrapped around his neck, choking off his air, and he fell to the floor once again. Two stools bounced off his prostrate body, and then the Sabellian went down beneath another mass attack.

"I've got to do *something!*" said Julius Squeezer apologetically. He raced to the cage, shoving aside the Gorbites as if they really were the animated Humpty Dumpties they looked like, and a moment later the huge wrestler was wreaking havoc within the cage itself.

Flint stood about fifty feet away, watching the round white bodies pouring out of the grandstand and half expecting to be attacked at any instant. He considered calling "Hey, Rube!" on the speaker system, but decided against it; if the carnies tried coming to the rescue and the fight spilled out from the cage to the rest of the tent, there would be no way to contain or stop it.

A pair of Gorbites suddenly noticed him, and he quickly threw a handful of sawdust in the first one's eyes and delivered a swift kick to the other. More surrounded him, and then, just before he could order the Dancer to fire into their midst, the Gorbite police showed up and began emptying the tent.

Flint sent Mr. Ahasuerus off to deal with them and pay whatever fines might be levied against the carnival. Then he walked over to the cage to assess the damage.

Batman was kneeling and blinking his eyes groggily. The Sabellian's body was bleeding from a score of wounds, and the jagged bone of his left forearm was jutting out through the skin. One of his ears was half severed, and his wing membranes seemed ripped almost beyond repair.

Monk lay on his back, blood coming out of his mouth, nose, and left ear. From the position of his legs, Flint guessed that both of them were broken. One of his fingers was bent at an impossible angle, and there was a horrible gurgling sound in his throat each time he breathed.

Julius Squeezer, appearing very little the worse for wear, was looking around helplessly, unable to decide what to do next.

"Thanks," said Flint, as he walked into the cage.

"I'm sorry, Thaddeus," said the wrestler. "But I couldn't just stand by and do nothing."

"You did fine," said Flint.

He walked over to Monk and squatted down next to him.

"Jupiter, this is Thaddeus. Can you hear me?"

Monk opened his swollen eyes. "I hope I'm alive," he mumbled through terribly mangled lips.

"You're alive," said Flint.

"Good. Because if I was dead and you were still around, I sure as hell couldn't be in heaven."

"Can you move?" asked Flint.

Monk winced. "I don't think so. It's my legs."

"I'll send for a stretcher," said Flint.

"No you won't," rasped the Sabellian, limping painfully over to Monk. "*I* will take him to the ship."

"You?" said Flint. "You're going to have enough trouble making it back by yourself."

"He is my partner," said Batman, spitting out a mouthful of blood. "I will care for him."

He bent over to reach for Monk, groaned and grabbed his rib cage, and collapsed in a heap.

Flint turned to Julius Squeezer. "Get two stretchers over here on the double." He looked at the Sabellian and shook his head. "Sure you'll help him, you stupid bat."

"Leave him alone, Thaddeus," said Monk weakly. "He's my partner."

Flint chuckled mirthlessly and sat down next to the two fallen performers to wait for the stretchers.

"Jesus, Thaddeus," mumbled Monk. "All we were ever gonna do was pull a couple of fast ones on the marks." He looked uncomprehendingly up at Flint. "How did it ever come to this?"

21.

Flint stopped by the infirmary a week later.

Both of Monk's legs were still in traction, but most of the bandages had been removed from his face. His left wrist was in a cast, and from the appearance of his hospital gown Flint assumed that his torso was still tightly wrapped. He was smoking a cigar and reading one of Tojo's less challenging novels.

Batman lay on a bed across the room. The right side of his head was still heavily bandaged following surgery on his ear, his left arm was in a sling, and his right leg had a cast extending from his ankle to his lower thigh. The bed had been jerry-rigged to accommodate his wing membranes, which Flint decided bore a striking resemblance to a circus tent that had been sewed up and patched together once too often. The Sabellian had an earphone plugged into his usable ear, but Flint couldn't tell what he was listening to, or even where the source was, since the cord disappeared beneath the starched sheets.

"Just thought I'd see how the combatants are doing," Flint announced, pulling a chair up next to Monk's bed.

"Getting by," said Monk, having some difficulty articulating because of the multitude of stitches that were still in his lips.

"Feeling any better?" asked Flint. "I came up here three or four days ago, and I don't think either one of you recognized me."

"Then I *must* be getting better," said Monk, starting to grin and then wincing with pain. "You look as ugly as ever."

"How about you?" asked Flint, turning to the Sabellian.

"I shall survive," replied Batman.

"That's what I like about you—you're always so damned cordial." Flint turned his attention back to Monk. "I talked to Fuzzy-Wuzzy a few minutes ago. He says you're going to have a permanent limp."

"Some doctor," muttered Monk.

"I don't think he's ever had to set a bone before," remarked Flint. "His specialty is yellow caterpillars. You ought to be grateful that he knew how to put you back together, even if he did glue a piece or two wrong."

"I am, Thaddeus," said Monk. "I'm just a little pissed at him today. He put me back on solids, and you know what my first goddamned meal was?"

"Green deathburgers?" asked Flint.

"Purple."

Flint smiled. "I don't know how to break this to you, but the galley is fresh out of lobster thermidor."

"Yeah? Well, the first thing I'm gonna do when I get out of here is take Fuzzy-Wuzzy down to the mess hall and shove a couple of those sandwiches down his yellow throat."

"Which brings up an interesting question," said Flint. "What's the *second* thing you're going to do?"

Monk tried to shrug, and found that he couldn't. "I don't know. The act is done with, if that's what you mean."

"Will you be wanting some more animals?"

"No, I don't think so. I couldn't work 'em right if I'm going to be limping all the time."

"Very good," said Flint. "I'm going to give you an eighty-five on that one."

"What are you talking about?"

"Jupiter, I've seen you stagger into the ring so drunk that you couldn't see an animal five feet away from you. So what's the real reason you're hanging it up?"

"It would bore me to tears," he said bluntly.

"Since when do lions and Red Devils bore you?"

"Since I learned what being in the cage with someone who can fight back is all about."

"And now you're all through with cages."

"Well, not exactly," said Monk.

"Oh?" said Flint, cocking an eyebrow.

"Batman and I have talked it over, and we've got a little proposition for you."

"Am I going to like it?"

"Probably not," admitted Monk.

"Good," said Flint. "I liked the last one, and look where it got us." He picked up Monk's cigar and began puffing on it. "Let's hear what you two geniuses have to say."

A moment later the three of them were lost in animated conversation.

22.

Four months had passed. The carnival was back on the galactic road, hopping from world to world for its brief playdates. Billybuck Dancer had returned to his accustomed slot in the specialty show, Diggs had added four more games to the Midway, and Julius Squeezer was on a tear, winning his last sixty-four matches.

"Things seem almost *too* calm these days," remarked Mr. Ahasuerus as he and Flint wandered down the Midway, checking the games and handling an occasional complaint from the marks.

"It takes some getting used to," admitted Flint, lighting up a cigarette. "I suppose I ought to be grateful that your idiot robots haven't learned how to brew a keg of beer yet, or I wouldn't have anything to complain about."

"You might try complaining about the price Kargennian gave us for our second specialty tent," said the blue man.

"Value received," grinned Flint. "One of these days he's going to figure out that we've still got the support poles."

"We do?" exclaimed Mr. Ahasuerus.

Flint nodded. "But don't worry. I'm sure you and the hotshot can hit upon an equitable price."

"I look forward to it with great anticipation."

"Didn't get your cappuccino machine yet, huh?"

"A bargain is a bargain," replied the blue man austerely.

They continued walking down the Midway, past

the games and the food stands and the tents and the rides, and finally they came to the Bozo cage.

Batman, no trace of emotion on his face, was sitting on a small platform about three feet above a tank of water, totally surrounded by the chain-link cage. To either side were plastic bull's-eyes, each attached to the platform by simple levers.

"I keep telling you, you dumb bastard!" Monk was yelling at him from a stand about fifty feet distant. "If you don't insult 'em, they ain't gonna spend their money."

"How about if he just insults *you*?" said Flint with a smile.

"Oh, hi, Thaddeus," said Monk. "You see that lazy son of a bitch up there? He gets dumped seventy or eighty times and suddenly he starts loafing on the job."

"Seventy or eighty times?" repeated Flint. "How much business have you two been doing?"

Monk flashed a huge wad of alien bills. "I don't know what they're worth, but we've been raking it in hand over fist." He turned to Batman. "No thanks to Bruce Wayne!" he bellowed.

While they were speaking a customer walked up, bought three throws for an equal number of bills, and hurled the first ball far off target.

"Excuse me a minute, Thaddeus," said Monk. He turned to the alien. "Look, son, you got it all wrong. You got to grip the ball like *this*."

The alien tried again, and came no closer.

"You don't listen real good, do you?" said Monk. He picked up a ball and hurled it at the bull's-eye. It struck its mark, and Batman's perch collapsed, hurling him into the water.

"See?" Monk grinned. "Nothing to it."

The alien waited until Batman had climbed back up, then hurled the third ball wildly.

"Idiot!" muttered Monk as the alien wandered away.

"Just how many of those dunks came from paying customers?" inquired Flint wryly.

"All of 'em," replied Monk, taking a bill out of one pocket and putting it in another. "When I throw, I pay." He raised his voice. "Not like some insensitive bastards I could name!"

"Enjoy yourself now," said the Sabellian coldly. "Tomorrow *you* will be in the cage."

"You couldn't hit the broad side of a barn," replied Monk with a laugh.

"We shall see," promised Batman.

"Yeah," said Flint as he and his partner continued their tour, "I'd say everything's back to normal again."

ABOUT THE AUTHOR

MIKE RESNICK was born in Chicago in 1942, attended the University of Chicago (where, in the process of researching his first adventure novel, he earned three letters on the fencing team and was nationally ranked for a brief period), and married his wife, Carol, in 1961. They have one daughter, Laura.

From the time he was 22, Mike has made his living as a professional writer. He and Carol have also been very active at science fiction conventions, where Mike is a frequent speaker and Carol's stunning costumes have swept numerous awards at masquerade competitions.

Mike and Carol were among the leading breeders and exhibitors of show collies during the 1970s, a hobby which led them to move to Cincinnati and purchase a boarding and grooming kennel.

Mike has received several awards for his short stories and an award for a nonfiction book for teenagers. His first love, though, remains science fiction, and his excellent science fiction novels—THE SOUL EATER, BIRTHRIGHT: THE BOOK OF MAN, WALPURGIS III, SIDESHOW, and THE THREE-LEGGED HOOTCH DANCER—are also available in Signet editions.